THE PERP WORE PUMPKIN II

A Humorous Crime Anthology

to

Benefit Second Harvest Food Bank

Edited by Sandra Murphy

****

White City

Press

A bad meal is a misdemeanor but going to bed hungry is the biggest crime of all.

Ten short story authors have joined forces to write humorous crime stories containing some of their favorite Thanksgiving dishes. From murder to theft to bank heists, these authors have whipped up stories to tickle your funny bone, feed your urge for a good crime and make you a bit hungry in the process. Not to be outdone, Lisa Lynn provides the perfect accompaniment with recipes that people can make for the holidays using the basic staples found in nearly every home or from your local food bank.

Thanks to the publisher's "Misti Gives Back" program, 100% of the net proceeds of the sales of this title will be split evenly among each of the contributors' local Second Harvest Food Bank (a member of Feeding America) to help raise money to feed those most in need and at risk. If a contributor does not have a Second Harvest in their area, their share will go directly to Feeding America. Your purchase(s) ensure that more people will have access to food this holiday season and beyond.

Paperback ISBN 9798866907649 eBook ISBN 9798868905124

Or directly from https://www.whitecitypress.com

THE PERP WORE PUMPKIN II

Edited by Sandra Murphy

First published by White City Press

An imprint of Misti Media LLC

https://www.whitecitypress.com

Available in both Paperback and eBook Editions

1 2 3 4 5 6 7 8 9 10

Acknowledgement

The following recipes are the property of, and copyrighted by, Lisa Lynn

Recipe for Easy Poultry, Rice and Carrot Soup

Recipe for Quick Black Beans

Recipe for Fruit Crumble

Contents

Talking Turkey — An Introduction
J. Alan Hartman

You would think that putting Thanksgiving food and crime together would be an easy feat to accomplish. In fact, I have plenty of experience in doing so. This time around, killing people with stuffing and stealing pumpkins feels a bit more important to me, and so added an extra layer of pressure.

Many years ago I created a series of books for another publisher that also mixed Thanksgiving and crime, and the series was (and, still is) quite successful. Having a humorous element to the stories was part of the appeal to bringing readers to the table, and over the course of six volumes I felt like I had created something fun that could almost be looked at as an annual Thanksgiving tradition.

This is all fine when you're creating something for profit, but my heart wanted to do more. If you have the ability to bring together amazingly talented authors to create an entertaining volume of writing, shouldn't you be using that to give something back?

I've always wanted to put together a charity anthology. As the world has experienced so much tragedy and aggravation over the last few years, a lot of charity funding has dried up and this has in turn hurt a lot of the communities that rely on the assistance.

The number of people who go to bed hungry every night is staggering. Food insolvency is a huge problem around the world. Food deserts exist where people have no access to fresh vegetables and other nutritious items. Poverty and changes in government assistance programs have made it harder than ever for people to be able to put food on the table. Inflation has drastically raised the prices of even basic staples necessary for preparing a meal. Therefore, more and more people are looking for help in feeding themselves and their families.

Organizations such as Second Harvest Food Bank and Feeding America do just that. Whether it's helping to operate food banks to provide sustenance to the hardest hit in the community, education programs or helping to push for legislation to make the situation better, these organizations are on the front lines of trying to end the food insolvency epidemic.

Thanksgiving foods and Second Harvest/Feeding America seemed like the perfect combination. I worried that moving forward with humorous crime stories might detract from the seriousness of these organizations' missions, but in the end realized that the more people I can…err…bring to the table, the bigger the benefit to the organization.

Thanks to the kind efforts of industry professionals (see our "Special Thanks to Our Co-Conspirators" section), we were able to reach our goal of donating 100% of the net sales of both the ebook and paperback editions of *The Perp Wore Pumpkin* to Second Harvest Food Bank locations in our authors' cities. If a contributor doesn't have a Second Harvest in their area, their portion will go to Feeding America. Misti Media will not keep a dime as part of our "Misti Gives Back" program.

Thanks for purchasing this title and for being part of the solution to food insolvency. Our little volume of stories may not change the world, but at least we know we took some positive action.

OK, enough with the serious stuff. Let's get back to killing people and robberies. You know, the fun stuff.

Jay Hartman

CEO/Editor-in-Chief

Misti Media, LLC

November, 2025

A Trifle Too Far
Shari Held

"You think Aunt Sadie will bring those god-awful pumpkin whoopie pies for Thanksgiving again this year, Dean?" Annabel asked.

"You know how she feels about family traditions, Sis."

"She did say she had a surprise for us. Maybe she's decided to bring something edible instead." Annabel muttered under her breath. "Please, please."

I cracked a smile. With Aunt Sadie—actually, she's our great-great Aunt Sadie—a surprise could mean anything from a moth-eaten beaver coat she'd won in a poker game to a new boyfriend she'd met at a senior yoga class. "We'll find out soon. Isn't that her fire-engine red Mustang speeding up the driveway?"

Aunt Sadie was in her nineties, but her mind and body hadn't yet received the message. I'm in my twenties and most of my girlfriends have less get-up-and-go. I pulled on my gray L.L. Bean fleece-lined sweatshirt and gloves and headed out in the brisk Indiana morning to help Aunt Sadie with her packages.

"Come here, Darlin'," Aunt Sadie cried as she gave me a bear hug. "You're a sight for sore eyes."

Her talon-like nails dug into my biceps and I backed off. The talons in question were painted white with squiggly lines in red and black and reminded me of snakes. I cringed. Annabel loves snakes—especially the two-legged kind. The thought of a snake slithering on its belly, its beady eyes, forked tongue and fangs headed toward me, turned my legs to jelly.

Aunt Sadie splayed her hands for me to admire.

I mustered up an appreciative tone. "Cool," I said and ducked into the car to grab her bags.

"Be careful not to disturb my pumpkin trifle on the floor of the front seat. I changed things up a bit this year." She mistook my look of relief for disappointment. "Don't worry. Instead of lady fingers, I substituted my famous pumpkin whoopie pies. No one will go without our traditional holiday fare."

I struggled to stifle a groan. Those things were deadly. Last year she'd made a special Oriental-style batch just for me, using fish sauce and pumpkin. It's a wonder I'm here to celebrate this Thanksgiving in our spankin' new gated-community McMansion.

Aunt Sadie stood in front of the red double-wide door to take in the two huge bittersweet wreaths, loaded with ribbons, corn husks, dried maple leaves, pinecones, faux gourds, and dried flowers and herbs. "It looks like a Stegosaurus vomited on your door," she said.

I chuckled. "If you think this is bad, wait 'til you see the inside. After Dad won the lottery, Effie couldn't wait to move out of our '70s tri-level. She hired a realtor the next day. She had the furniture ordered and ready for delivery on Day One and has been 'styling' the house ever since. She calls it 'safari chic.' I call it 'jungle jumble.'"

Aunt Sadie rolled her eyes. "Guess I'd better go in and act like I give two hoots about what your stepmother has done with the house. I'm sure she'll be happy to give me the royal tour."

"Wait," I said. "The McMansion has some peculiarities—one you need to know about. The previous owner had an intercom system installed. From their bedroom, Dad and Effie can tune in to all the bedrooms, the great room, and the library. If you want to say something you'd prefer Effie wouldn't hear, whisper or write it out."

"Noted, Dean. Thanks for the intel."

I grinned as I opened the door and shouted, "Hey, everyone. Aunt Sadie's here."

"I've brought a special treat this year," she said. "Pumpkin trifle."

She held the whipped cream topped trifle high over her head. Light glinted off the peacock-decorated, iridescent carnival glass bowl. "This is a new twist on my traditional pumpkin whoopie pies."

I placed the trifle in our turquoise Sub-Zero designer fridge and joined everyone in the great room, which was about as livable as a prison cell.

Two white upholstered sofas faced one another on either side of the gigantic fireplace. A zebra-print carpet covered most of the wood floor. A rectangular glass coffee table supported by plaster busts of some long-dead dudes sat between the sofas. In the middle of the room stood a thirteen-foot black giraffe. A crystal chandelier dangled from its mouth.

Dad refused to give up his battered brown tweed recliner when we moved to our new home. Effie placed it to one side of a sofa near a fake palm tree with far-reaching fronds. That chair sparked more fireworks between her and Dad than anything—even me.

Effie grouped the rest of the great room into what she calls "conversation areas." In one, she'd had wingback chairs covered with patterned brown leather and exotic tiger-striped hide. The other one was decorated using leather director chairs with leopard-print pillows, a side table of a leopard holding a tray, and assorted safari furniture. The place gave me the creeps.

The women were seated on the sofas. The men placed the accent chairs near the loveseats so everyone could sit together. I sniggered as my older brother Joe struggled to fit his fat ass into one of the director chairs.

Effie pounced on Aunt Sadie before she could even sit. "Come, let me give you the grand tour." Effie used her best lady-of-the-manor voice.

"Certainly, Effie. I've been dying to see everything." Aunt Sadie winked at me as Effie led her out of the room. The rest of us traded digs and snide remarks. Joe and I bet on how long our other brother's second marriage would last. Chuck glared at us, then pulled Elizabeth onto his lap and put a lip lock on her while giving us the finger.

Aunt Sadie and Effie had no sooner returned to the great room when the doorbell rang. "Who could that be?" Dad asked. "We don't know anyone in the neighborhood—and it's Thanksgiving. Everyone should be with family on Thanksgiving."

Effie hustled to the door as fast as four-inch high heels would allow. I followed, just out of curiosity. Two men were on the porch. The tall one was dressed in a black Stetson and red cowboy boots while the shorter one wore a Dallas Cowboys ballcap over his manbun.

"Excuse me, ma'am," Manbun said. "I'm Burt and this here is Homer. We only found out about you when our great grandma died. We're your cousins, four times removed. Thought we'd drive up here from Texas to visit with you all on Thanksgiving."

Effie stared at them as if they were little green men with giant eyes in the middle of their foreheads. She turned to Dad, who, like me, had come to see who was at the door. "Harold, does that sound right to you?"

"Pretty sure they're not from my side of the family, but they could be from the Graham side. If anyone knows, it will be Aunt Sadie. She pays attention to that kind of thing." He beckoned for the men to follow him. "Come on in, you two. I'll introduce you to everyone. Sorry, but I didn't catch your last name."

"Graham," Burt said.

Dad introduced Annabel, my brothers Joe and Chuck and their wives, Cousin Kate, and Aunt Sadie.

"So, Sadie, could they be from your side of the family?" Dad asked.

Aunt Sadie walked around them, inspected them carefully. "You're from Texas, you say?"

Both men nodded.

Aunt Sadie furrowed her brow. "Well, seems like Alice was in Texas for a spell. She liked her cowboys. Made a beeline for anything with a bulge in its crotch. Then she'd disappear for a year or two at a time. I suppose they could be hers."

Effie resumed her role as lady of the manor. "Well, whoever you are, you're welcome to join us for our Thanksgiving meal and stay in one of our guestrooms overnight while we figure it out. We have more than enough food and rooms."

"Don't mind if we do, ma'am," Burt said.

They brought their duffel bags inside. We all sat around in the great room while the Thanksgiving turkey cooked in the Thermador convection oven. Maybe, like the ads proclaimed, the new appliance would cook our turkey to perfection. Effie sure couldn't. If our guests' expectations of our Thanksgiving meal were based on our fancy house, they were in for a disappointment.

With the two newly found relatives present, everyone was extra polite. Even the women, who got along about as well as cats and mice. I knew this good behavior wouldn't last. I didn't expect it to be Burt who got things back to normal.

Burt squeezed himself on a sofa next to Annabel. His face made it clear he'd like to be more than kissing cousins. I didn't like the way he ogled her chest. Before I could catch his attention, he'd leaned into her and wolf-whistled in the direction of her girls. She yelped, jumped up, and moved to sit on Dad's chair arm.

Every head in the room turned toward Burt.

"No offense," he said, raising both hands. "I can't resist admiring a nice pair when I see them." He winked at Annabel who grimaced and looked away.

Before I could clock him one, Joe's wife, Sallie, chimed in. "What about mine? I'm a 36D. She pulled back her shoulders and waited to be admired. "My boobs are better than hers, don't you think so, Joe?"

Joe was saved when Cousin Kate snorted. "Yours are certainly more expensive. How much did they cost you?"

"More than your bargain basement boobs," Sallie said.

Cousin Kate glared at her with laser eyes and clenched her fists.

Chuck's wife Elizabeth, the quiet one in the bunch, snickered, gulped the last of her Carlo Rossi, then pulled off her prim and proper boxy blazer, tugged her top to lower the neckline and revealed a cleavage that rivaled anything I'd ever seen that wasn't on the big screen. "I've got you all beat."

"Damn." I whistled my appreciation. "Who knew?"

Chuck scowled, Joe stifled a laugh, and Dad's face turned red as Aunt Sadie's Mustang. Our two guests looked as if they were having a high old time with their new relatives.

Never one to be quiet, Aunt Sadie spoke up. "Now, ladies, stop this undignified discussion right now. We all know size doesn't matter."

"I wonder which guy told her that?" I whispered to Joe, who spit his beer all over his yellow sweater.

Effie excused herself to check on the meal. Sallie, Elizabeth, Cousin Kate, Annabel, and Aunt Sadie followed her cue.

"Mighty fine digs you have here," Burt said, unconcerned he'd caused a commotion. "I wouldn't turn down a walk-through if it was offered." His smile was as sleazy as his red bandana-print Western shirt.

I smelled a skunk, and it wasn't black, white, and furry. "Sure," I said. "We have plenty of time before dinner. How about I show you two to the guestroom first so you can get settled. I'll drop back in fifteen or twenty minutes to give you the tour."

* * *

I've never led a home tour before. Not exactly my thing, but I figured I could do a good enough job for those two. Besides, I wanted to see what interested them. Plus, if Effie found out, she'd be pissed—an added bonus. "We don't have everything furnished or finished yet," I said, as I led Burt and Homer around the house. I thought Homer was going to jump into the indoor pool, clothes and all. Fortunately, he didn't. Burt, on the other hand, seemed more intent on the master suite and the library. He lagged behind and I caught him as he peeked behind a painting in the library. The one that hid the safe. I ducked out so he wouldn't see me and joined Homer. I knew it. Our so-called cousins were crooks.

We ended back at the guestroom, so they could get ready for dinner.

I scurried into Dad's bedroom and pushed the intercom button to their guestroom.

"Lucky thing we struck up a conversation with that contractor back at the diner," Burt said. "We owe him a big thank you for telling us this family paid him thousands of dollars in cash. I bet there's more where that came from and it's in neat little stacks waiting for me to get my hands on it. While I crack the safe, you create a distraction. I'd rather not use the guns. We'll grab the money, make an excuse to leave, and be in Ohio before they know they've been hit. Got it?"

"Got it." Homer said. "I cooked up a great idea to keep them entertained. Are you sure we need to do this before we eat? I wouldn't mind some turkey and fixins."

"With duffel bags stuffed with money, we'll be able to eat anything and anywhere we want."

I'd heard enough. My instincts were right on. I love Dad, but he's not the brightest bulb. If I told him, he'd want to confront them. We guys outnumbered them, but they had guns. Guns trump one unarmed overweight senior, one flabby son, and two lightweights. It was up to me and Annabel to deal with Homer and Burt.

* * *

I hurried to the kitchen and pulled Annabel aside.

"These guys are worse than freeloaders," I said. "I caught Burt searching under the painting in the library. He found the safe. He's going to crack it and steal the cash while Homer distracts us. They've got guns. We've got to do something."

Annabel's face turned pale, then she stomped her foot. "Those scumbags. Aunt Sadie was so excited to think we found another branch of the family tree. It's all she's talked about. You need to come up with a chore, ask if they will help you. Like now. While they're doing that, I'll boobytrap the safe for our dear *cousins*. I know where Dad keeps the code."

"Why don't you stash the money in a suitcase and hide it under the bed?"

"Do you know how many bills there will be? With my luck, I'd get it packed up right in time to hand it over to them."

"I see what you mean. How about I ask them to help me carry in the drinks from the garage refrigerator? That should give you about ten minutes."

We barely finished replenishing the drinks in the Sub-Zero, when Annabel came into the kitchen, a big smile on her face. Burt and Homer excused themselves but promised to congregate with everyone in the formal dining room in a few minutes.

The previous owners left the dining room furnished, and Effie hadn't been able to put her mark on it in time for Thanksgiving. For that alone, I gave thanks on this holiday. Next year, who knows? We might have to choke down our Thanksgiving spread across the room from a saber-toothed tiger or a polar bear. Currently, although it was a little over the top, the dining room was the most normal-looking room in the McMansion.

A ginormous Italian crystal chandelier hung smackdab in the center of the ceiling, while smaller ones were at either end. A huge granite-topped sideboard sat on one side of a massive, polished mahogany dining table, while a glass front floor-to-ceiling China cabinet stood opposite.

"Dean, tell the guys in the great room to head to the dining room," Aunt Sadie said.

"Will do," I replied. I corralled the guys, then proceeded to the kitchen to help carry dishes to the table. I had mashed potatoes, Annabel brought the cranberry salad, and Aunt Sadie held on tight to her pumpkin trifle.

Before we made it into the dining room, Homer burst into the kitchen dressed in his cowboy boots, hat, tighty whities, and nothing else. He stomped around in circles as if he were doing a Native American rain dance, yelled gibberish, and brandished a gun pointed toward the ceiling. I wondered if the gun was loaded or just for show.

I found out soon enough. Homer pulled the trigger while he faced the dining room. The bullet took down the central crystal chandelier and spewed glass shards all over the table.

Dad, Joe, and Chuck dropped to the floor as Homer let off another round. This one shattered the China cabinet. Sallie, Kate, and Elizabeth ran from the kitchen to the garage.

"Noooo," Effie screamed, as she grabbed a carving knife from the kitchen counter and ran at Homer. Her face was screwed up so much, her eyes were the size of raisins. "You ingrate! We invite you into our home and this is the thanks we get? By the time I get through with you, you'll be thankful to be alive!"

Homer did what every red-blooded young man would do with a menopausal madwoman on his tail. He turned on the heel of one cowboy boot to dash down the hall.

And collided with Burt.

Burt was hightailing it to the kitchen, arms stretched out, head turned to look behind him. "Copperhead! Big one!" He jumped onto the kitchen table, his knees knocking together. His eyes were glued on the snake.

Sure enough, a red, black, and tan snake slithered down the hallway, making a beeline for Homer, who yelled and turned toward me, Annabel, and Aunt Sadie who sacrificed her precious trifle. She held the bowl high and smashed it on Homer's head. He dropped his gun and staggered to a chair, remembered to pull his legs up on the seat to avoid the snake.

"Yuck," Homer said, as he licked trifle off his face. "This is the worst stuff ever."

Aunt Sadie, her face a thunderbolt, shook his chair, a threat to tip it over. I've never heard a grown man squeal like Homer did then. "I broke one of my favorite bowls because of you," Aunt Sadie said. "Not to mention destroyed my Thanksgiving trifle. Now shut your trap or I'll have Annabel wrap that snake around your neck so you can dance for us again."

Annabel had booby-trapped the safe, all right. Turns out Burt and

Homer were as snake-a-phobic as I am. I was so involved with what was going on I forgot to be afraid until the excitement was over. I was relieved when Annabel picked up Big Red, her pet Eastern milk snake, and carried him to his aquarium in her room.

Dad, Joe, and Chuck wasted no time in tying Burt and Homer to the kitchen chairs while Effie called the police.

When the cops arrived, the two Texans admitted they planned to steal Dad's lottery winnings. The police made Homer get dressed before they took the pair to the station. No one else should have to see what we did.

"Those two could have stolen all our money," Effie said after they left and only family was gathered in the grand room. I could swear I saw a tear trickle down the side of her face.

Dad patted her knee. "No way. You don't think I'd leave our money lying around in the safe, do you? That's the first place thieves look."

"So, Dad," I asked, "where *did* you hide the money?"

"Somewhere no one would suspect." He sat there, a smug look on his face, waited for us to plead with him to spill his secret.

Finally, he held up his hands. "Okay. I hid our money in the potting shed in boxes marked rat poison and pesticides. No one wants to get around that stuff."

"Dad," I asked, "how many boxes did it take?"

"Oh, about four skids."

Like that wouldn't stand out if someone really searched the house and grounds. Who needs that much rat poison?

I think Dad went a trifle too far this time.

And a Thanksgiving Turkey Named John Glenn

Sandra Murphy

Ronnie and Buddy sat in Buddy's beat-up, back-up, surveillance car in the strip mall lot where they could see who went in and out of one store in particular, hopefully without anyone noticing them.

"How long are we going to be here?" Ronnie tried to stretch but was too tall to find the room. "Cletus is deep frying turkeys starting today, gotta get ahead of the orders. We missed out last year, thanks to you."

"Like it was my fault I got shot? If you'd moved nice and smooth, like I taught you, I'd have had a clear path to my perp, but no…Old Man Henderson had to save your sorry butt. I was fine."

"You were laid out on the floor, head in Sharon's lap, lettin' her fuss all over you. Look where *that* got us!" Ronnie took a few photos with his phone. "Sittin' on this store when we could be watching Cletus and them fryers, in case one of them barrels of oil shoots a turkey into orbit. Quit your grinnin'. I don't know why I hadda come along."

"Is that your new accent? Which girlfriend is this one for? I gotta say, it's better than that fake British you tried out on, uh, Janeene, was it?"

"It was my Paul Hollywood voice. She was into that Netflix baking show but she couldn't bake worth a darn. I'm not hookin' up with somebody who can't make a pie." Ronnie tried to shift in his seat again, to no avail. "Come on. We ain't got all day. There's only so much stakin' out we can do. We gotta go in."

"A few more minutes?"

"You sound like a five-year-old wantin' to avoid going to bed because monsters are gonna to eat you. Get a move on. We're doin' this." Ronnie opened the passenger car door and eased himself into a standing, stretching position. "Now!"

"Maybe there aren't monsters, but I wish there was." Buddy took a couple of deep breaths and with a determined look in his eyes, he crossed the parking lot to the store. Once there, he stood to one side of the door and when anyone went in or out, he tried to look nonchalant. Mostly he looked sick. It got him two sympathetic nods, three sneers, and one customer did a U-turn right back inside.

"We've been made." Ronnie sighed. "You couldn'ta been more obvious."

"Me? You're the one built like the Hulk. I blend into the background."

"You two! With me, get in here, now."

One look at the stern-faced woman and the two men meekly followed her inside. Both glanced around. Surrounded by mountains of pale yellows, minty greens, clouds of soft pinks, and sky-toned blues, they forgot how to speak.

"Let's see who's who here." She gave both the once-over. "You, you look like you've been struck dumb and that wasn't a big jump." The comment was aimed at Ronnie. She turned to Buddy. "Yep, you're the one. You're just as dumb but also in a full-blown panic. Give me the list, then go sit down, behave yourselves. I'll tell you when we need you."

Buddy fished several pages of paper from his shirt pocket. Ronnie handed over a list too.

One more stern look and they sat.

"What's with the second list? I've got enough on mine to start a store myself."

"Rose, Amy, the new girl, Carol, some of their favorite customers, all gave me their lists. Sharon sure is popular."

"She's a doll." Buddy had a sappy grin that just about ate up his face.

"A whole year and you still got it bad. Good for you. And now this."

Ronnie's vision seemed to come back into focus as he looked around. "Good grief, who knew a baby needed so much merch?"

"I didn't even know what half the stuff on the list was and I was too scared to ask. Ronnie, I'm not ready to be a dad. You gotta know how to do stuff with a kid. The last kid I knew was me!" Buddy was about to hyperventilate.

A hand reached over his shoulder. "Breathe into this. You'll be fine."

He took the paper lunch bag and did as he was told until his panic passed. "Right, no matter what, the important thing is Sharon and the baby are healthy and happy. I can do this."

"Damn straight."

"Stop cussin'. I don't want my kid's first word to be damn."

* * *

One call to Rent-a-U-Haul, two hours, and three Dr Peppers later, Buddy drove to the Eat In-Carry Out where Sharon used to work as a server, one of the best, Buddy always said. Carol, the newest server, was there alone, the restaurant closing early for the day on account of Sharon's surprise baby shower and Cletus deep frying the turkeys, always a perilous job. He was a careful man but due to demand for deep fried turkeys, this year he had helpers, trained of course. Still, he worried. That old saying about 'too many cooks' came from someone's bad experience.

The Eat In-Carry Out crew were in their element. After years of decorating the eatery for customer's parties, now it was their turn. They pulled out the stops with balloons, streamers, miniature cakes, pies, cookies, and a homemade ice cream machine was cranking out flavors by the gallon.

"Buddy, how're you gonna get Sharon here? I thought she was sticking close to home lately." A woman Buddy recognized but whose name he blanked on yelled across the room.

"I convinced her we should have a do over on Thanksgiving memories. This year would be nice and calm. We could forget last year's fiasco. She did make me promise, no lemon meringue pie this time. I can get one to take home though." Buddy's mouth watered at the thought.

As usual, Old Man Henderson sat at the counter, last stool on the right. Buddy wasn't sure the guy ever went home. "Howya doin' there, Mr. Henderson? Got the crossword all done?"

Generally a man of few words, he nodded, shoved the newspaper aside, and held up a paperback book to show the cover, some kind of cookbook with a cake on the cover.

"I didn't know you were into baking. Is it something new for you?"

"Crime stories with food as the theme. Some dandy tales, just published."

"Sounds good. Happy Thanksgiving. We'll see you tomorrow at the shower."

Henderson just nodded and went back to his book.

"You sure lucked out, getting shot and all. Old Man Henderson proposed to Sharon every Saturday like clockwork. He would have worn her down sooner or later and she'd have said yes."

Buddy almost choked on a mini pecan pie. "Like hell she would!"

"Who's usin' cuss words now?" Ronnie stood. "Let's go check on Cletus and them turkeys."

* * *

Engine #4 was on hand in case of flaming, orbiting turkeys and any sparks that could lead to brush fires. Cletus drew quite a crowd, all behind barriers so everyone could see what was happening but keep out of the danger zone. Tables were set up for chess or card players, kids rolled down the hillside, patrol officers kept any squabbles to just that, no fighting allowed. Moms sat at tables shaded by patio umbrellas and sipped fruity drinks. No one checked to see if relaxing additives of the alcoholic variety had been added.

Buddy was confused but that seemed to be his usual state lately. "What the hell are they doing with that big tree limb?" He pointed to the restaurant's back door as several people, mainly two in control of the limb and half a dozen 'advisors' tried to get through the narrow opening without destroying the leafy branch. "It's a mini tree."

"Money tree." One of the slushy-drinking moms overheard and slurred the information.

It sounded like mini tree to Buddy and Ronnie. "That's what I just said."

"Since Sharon doesn't know or won't tell the sex of the baby, no one knows what to get as a gift. They'll fold paper money like a baby's diaper and hang it on the tree." She turned and shouted, "Another round for my girls!"

"I don't think that's the first time she's called for another round. She and 'her girls' may regret it tomorrow, but I can't blame them. Having everything barricaded is like free babysitting and the Dads won't complain about being here."

"Let's see what we can do with this tree thing." Buddy and Ronnie provided more unneeded, unwanted advice, until the limb finally gave up and went inside, peacefully intact.

Buddy was sent home early with several to-go dinners and instructions to make sure Sharon rested. Ronnie stayed behind, not so much to work on the decorations but more to flirt and dance with Grandma Rose which endeared him to all the single ladies.

* * *

The next morning, Buddy managed to get away from the house by calling his neighbor, Barb, to come over for a visit. Sharon had been restless all night and needed to settle down but Buddy was no help in that regard. Barb had a way about her that naturally calmed folks. It was a plus that Barb was a nurse. Just in case.

The baby store employees had a system of keeping track of who gifted what. There was a small sticker for each package that gave the name of the item and the gifter so there would be no mix-ups. Given the quantity of gifts Buddy'd seen, it would be a time saver to be sure.

It was almost noon, opening time for the holiday, when Buddy walked into the Eat In-Carry Out to discover a true catastrophe, at least in the eyes of the shower's organizers and the restaurant owners. A beat cop was on hand to take names and statements. Buddy overheard a radio call asking for detectives.

Ronnie saw him come in and wove through the crowd.

"What in the hell is going on? Tell me this isn't a replay of last year. I don't see any lemon meringue pie on the floor." Buddy could barely hear over the voices all chattering at once.

"You remember that mini tree?"

"Money tree? Sure, I'm not senile yet and it was only yesterday that we helped drag it in here. Speaking of that, where is it? We set it up over where everybody picks up to-go orders." Buddy scanned the room. Nope, it hadn't relocated on its own.

"The tree limb is out back. The money? Disappeared. Quite a haul too. I'm told a lot of people hung twenties and fifties on it after I left. That was about an hour after you bailed."

"I bailed? You were dancing with Grandma Rose and making googly eyes at all the single women. I don't need to see that kind of thing. You're the one who told me to skedaddle." Buddy gave Ronnie a one-finger poke to the chest. He could always get away with one but never dared to try a second poke. It would be too much like poking a bear.

"Well, anyways, the damn thing was out back when the first people got here, about half hour before I did. They figure there was a couple thousand dollars on it. You got generous friends. Or should I say, Sharon's got generous friends? All *you* got is me, lucky I put up with you, what with getting' shot and all."

"Knowin' somebody who's willing to take a bullet for you has only improved your status. Deal with it." Buddy scanned the room. "I see Reynolds is taking statements. Who're they sending to detect? I hope it's not Harris."

"You hope in vain. Harris and a new gal, Wilson. On their way."

"So, how do you want to play this? Wander around and eavesdrop? Herd everybody outside where the perp could hide the dough? Stay *in here* where the perp could hide the dough? I figure any way we go, the money's gone." Buddy scanned the crowd. "I thought maybe teenagers acting on a dare, but they're obsessed with the turkeys. We're lookin' for an adult."

"One that's not too bright either. Who else would be stupid enough to steal money from a detective and his brilliant partner?" Ronnie grinned.

"I know you think you're the brilliant partner but that's my claim to fame. You can ride along with your good looks. I'll give you that much. Let's split up and see what we can see."

* * *

Ronnie wandered through the restaurant, smiling but always looking for anything out of place. There were just too many people. Either someone asked for help with crepe paper streamers that wouldn't stay twisted overhead or a well-meaning friend would encourage him to eat 'a little something.' Some of the women tried to bribe him into telling the sex of the baby.

Buddy wasn't having any better luck outside. He corralled little ones who wandered away from their moms, warned teens about smoking near hot grease, convinced at least two drunks that no, you do not pour beer into the cavity of the turkey before dropping it into hot oil. A couple of other beer lovers had to be warned to either go inside for a bathroom break or choose taller shrubbery to hide behind. Maybe the booing from the ladies would be discouragement enough.

"Buddy, did you see anything?"

"Boy, did I! Some things I just don't think you can unsee but I'm trying. No clues though. What say we just skip the whole thing and let the police detectives worry about it."

"What about our reputations as whiz private detectives? I don't want the suits to outdo us."

"Hey, we've got the baby shower excuse and non-success can't be held against us. Sharon would never forgive me if I got shot again."

"Wouldn't forgive me either. I'm supposed to watch out for you. She said you have baby brain and might do something stupid like walk into a parking meter or something." Ronnie smirked. "I'd pay to see that, but she'd be after me so better skip it for now."

"It's time for me to go pick her up anyway. You staying or coming with?"

"Chocolate pecan pie is calling my name. I'll stay put, see what I can see."

* * *

It seemed to Buddy that getting Sharon out of the house, into the car, without twelve 'oh, wait, I forgot', 'better make one more trip to the bathroom', and 'did you bring my bag, just in case' comments were taking longer than any trip they were taking. The Eat In-Carry Out was only fifteen minutes from their house. It took forty-five minutes to get there.

Getting out of the car and into the restaurant was another fifteen minutes. "Are they serving today? I thought you said it was just to deep fry the turkeys. I'm not sure why I need to see that. Plus, my back hurts. Oh, I'm being such a drag, and on a holiday too. I want today to be nice, to wipe out last year's Thanksgiving." Sharon looked near tears, a common sight lately.

"I guess people are picking up their turkeys and pies. Watch your step here. You can sit as soon as we get inside. We're on the countdown now."

"Okay, honey. I hope there's cherry pie. I love cherry. And blackberry."

Buddy opened the door to the foyer, and then into the restaurant—and wisely got out of the way as a roar of congratulations and shouts of 'surprise' rolled over them. In shock, Sharon stood, open mouthed for a minute, and then burst into tears. She was immediately surrounded by friends who ushered her to the most comfortable chair, closest to the gifts. "Oh my goodness, the baby will be in high school by the time I can finish opening so many wonderful gifts."

Buddy thought it best to relocate himself, somewhere farther from the bows stuck to paper plates, wrapping and tissue paper accumulation. Ronnie was near the back door, where he could see but not be seen.

"It's been quiet, but I swear something's up. The teenagers are looking sneaky and spacing themselves out instead of hanging in a clump like usual. I warned the fire guys to watch them. No progress on the mini tree and all the big bucks. Quite a few guys looked shifty, but they were spiking their coffees with whiskey, like no one figured that out. You got any ideas?"

"Not a one. I'm ready for a nap. I don't know how Sharon does it. It takes a complete battle plan to get from the house to the car." Buddy sighed. "We better get inside. Sharon will think we're not interested in onesies."

"Are we?"

"If we know what's good for us, we are."

There was already a lull in the gift opening as Sharon made another trip to the bathroom. Ronnie took the opportunity to make his way to the mini chocolate pecan pies again. Buddy grabbed a beer, promised himself it would be the only one.

The crowd quieted some, just in time to hear the distinct sound of a hard slap and ensuing cry of pain. Ronnie and Buddy moved as one toward the server's station. Carol and an unknown man were there, her cheek a bright red in the shape of a hand, his face red from anger.

"You can't do this. These are my friends. I won't let you rob them." Carol's voice was weak but determined.

"What're you going to do to stop me? I'll tell your boss you've been skimming tips. Then what? Who's he going to believe?"

"I haven't taken a dime that wasn't mine and you know it!"

"Give me the bag or you can forget coming home. Who'll have anything to do with you except me? I only do it because I feel sorry for your ugly self." He raised his fist to hit harder this time.

Before Buddy and Ronnie could move, there was another cry. "Not at my shower, you big jackass!" A sugar shaker flew and hit the back of the man's head. He went down like a puppet whose strings had been cut.

Buddy turned to see Sharon grab the back of a chair. "Buddy, he was going to ruin my lovely party." Her face paled to white. "I think we need to go. Now."

"Go? Go where?"

"Ronnie, drive Buddy to the hospital, will ya?" Old Man Henderson moved to Sharon's side faster than anyone thought he could move. "One of you guys run out back and tell the ambulance driver he's got a passenger and he better hurry. Tell the detective to get in here and arrest that jackass on the floor. He done stole the baby money."

"What's happening?" Buddy didn't know where to look, who to listen to right now.

"Baby's coming, get a move on."

Ronnie grabbed Buddy's arm and dragged him out to the car. "We'll wait for the ambulance to pull out and then ride their wake to the hospital."

In just a few minutes, they could see the flashing red lights and got ready to fall in behind. Siren blaring, the ambulance roared out of the parking lot.

Ronnie put the car in gear. Whump! The windshield spidered into multiple cracks. "What the hell?"

A partially cooked deep fried turkey, one leg now impaled through the windshield, had achieved orbit and landed on Buddy's beat-up, back-up, surveillance car.

* * *

The pair raced into the hospital, thanks to a ride from the new detective. "Are we in time? Did we miss it?"

"You've still got time for the second one. First one is doing fine." The nurse smiled but had to grab Buddy's arm to keep him upright.

"What do you mean, first?"

"I thought you knew. You're having twins. I'll let Sharon tell you who's who."

* * *

"Honey, I'm not sure we'll ever have a normal Thanksgiving. Maybe we should just embrace the weirdness of it all. We'll have stories to tell our grandkids."

"Buddy, let's get through day one of kids before you populate the world with grandkids." Sharon was exhausted but all smiles. "Is it okay with you that I picked the boy's name?"

"Of course, what did you decide?"

"David. Maybe Carol for the girl?"

"Where did David come from?"

"From me," a deep voice answered. Old Man Henderson.

"That's your name? I never knew."

"I keep a low profile." The old man grinned. "Get used to it. I'm part of the family now."

"Then I guess we should get a photo. Gather round."

"Our first photo for the family album." Sharon smiled.

"Do you think we need to name the turkey?" Ronnie reached for another mini chocolate pecan pie. "It only seems polite."

Ronnie, Old Man Henderson, Buddy, Sharon, the two babies (David and Carol), and a half-cooked deep-fried turkey named John Glenn smiled for the camera.

"Say Mini-Me!"

Choked on Love
Kevin R. Tipple

"Billy Bob, I appreciate the invite and all, but I'm not coming to Thanksgiving this year. I'm staying here. I got a turkey breast and some taters, gravy from a jar, and I am good. I've got books. I've got football. Dude, I'm good."

"Come on, Leroy. You need to get out of that house."

"Nope."

The Saturday before Thanksgiving. I looked at my tv where College Game Day was in Austin. That overheated fraternity boy moron was standing up and waving at the crowd. I had the talking heads on mute as they offered their takes on who would win, and the gambling odds scrolled on each game. I had to give Leroy credit. He could drink. I was pretty sure his liver hated him.

He let loose a belch that damn near ruptured my ear drum and then said, "Listen, it won't be like last year."

I pulled the phone away as he belched again. Not as bad as the first, but my ear was still feeling the effects of the last one. Now I knew he was at least three beers in today. Once he was three beers in, he could belch on command, and make the belches sound like words. When he was sufficiently lubricated, he could do entire sentences. What was funny a couple of decades ago was just kind of sad now. The Longhorns had the noon kickoff, and I wanted to watch so I really wanted to wrap this up.

"I would hope not. Hey, is Jimmy out of jail yet?"

"Nope."

"Aunt Barbara called the other night and said he got picked up for something and there went his bond."

"Yep."

Leroy was suddenly not talking so I knew something was up. I decided to push as Leroy might tell me something and then decide to get off the phone. It was always better if he bailed first on the phone call.

"You know what he did now, Leroy?"

"Nope. Knowing Jimmy, it had to be something stupid. That boy is all barn and no hay."

"Don't I know it." I heard a can get crushed and then, a couple of seconds later, the top snap open on the next. Leroy was hard at work and it still wasn't noon.

"So, he isn't coming and neither is Stella. It would be Ashley, the Thompson Twins, and Old Man Hubbard from next door. You know his wife died last year from that Chinese flu thing, so this is his first one alone. I figured I better get him over here and feed him as that man is grieving really bad. You and he have a lot in common if you ignore the age gap between you two."

I was not going to rise to that bait. There was no limit on how long to grieve as I found out damn near every day. *Enough of that.* Nobody cared.

"Well, I appreciate the offer, but I think I'm going to take a pass."

"Okay, fine. I am a grown man and I'm not going to beg. If you change your mind, just come on, as there will be plenty."

"Sure thing."

I'm not sure he even heard me as he loudly belched again and hung up. I sat back in my natty recliner and briefly contemplated my circle was so small these days it was either go to Billy Bob's and hang out with his flock of misfits or hang at the house, heat up my stuff, and watch crappy football. At least I had a new *Ed Earl Burch* book to read and I knew that would be way better than the football games.

I sighed aloud and shook my head as my mind drifted back to

Thanksgiving last year. Leroy had pushed hard for me to come. I wanted no part of it, but the man had been relentless. The push this year was pretty tame.

At one point, he'd threatened to make the hour drive, kick in my door, bag me, and take me back with him. He hunted a lot and the big man worked out constantly so I was pretty sure he could, if he wanted to, truss me up like a mule deer, bodily carry me out to his 4x4, and haul me the hour plus drive to his backwoods place. Just to get him to shut up, I finally agreed to go. Over strenuous objections, I insisted I would drive myself. I figured if I had my own car I could flee if it all got to be too much. I didn't want to be relying on somebody else to bring me home.

So, I'd made the hour plus long drive out to Leroy's place. Fall had come late, and the trees were prettier than normal. The drive had been decent and I had kind of enjoyed it.

Despite my misgivings, things at dinner had been mostly okay. Everybody had, somehow, stayed off politics, and even left me alone about my situation, and in general had behaved themselves. The food was pretty good too. Everything had pretty much been fine, but it was too good to last. We didn't even make it to dessert.

Stella started choking on a forkful of stuffing. Jimmy, with all the brains of a rabid squirrel, thought this could be best solved by poking her in her ribs and tickling her. So, he got up and started doing so with a hand on each side of her ribcage. He leaned over her to do it, and she coughed and choked harder. He was still leaning over her when she managed to rise straight up out of her chair fast and hard enough that she powered into his jaw.

"Damn, woman!" he swore at her as he took a couple of steps backwards and managed to break a half dozen plates in the hutch. He got himself straightened up and then sort of slapped at her as she stumbled around away from the table. Of course, part of the reason she stumbled, beyond the whole choking thing, was because her chair was over on its back with the legs right where she was moving.

By this point, Aunt Thelma, who had been next to her on one side of the table and across from me, while Jimmy sat next to her, decided she needed to get up and do something. Her effort consisted of patting stumbling Stella on the shoulder and saying "There, there" like Stella was a crying baby. That wasn't doing anything as Stella's face got redder and her blue eyes started to look like they were going to bug out of her skull.

I'd seen the Heimlich maneuver at a demonstration at the county library a few weeks back. I'd been supposed to try it on the dummy the Visiting Nurses Association had brought in for the group to practice on, but the thing had broken long before it was my turn. Still, I sort of knew what to do, so I got up and went around the table to help her.

Cousin Jimmy got in my way, so I hip checked him again as I had in the football game we played outside before dinner and got my hands on her. She was in mid-spin as she staggered around, half bent over. I slipped my hands in her armpits and yanked back as I told her to stand up. She sort of straightened, though she was squirming around with her arms flailing around like one of those tube deals outside of a used car place while Leroy yelled, "Girl, act right. He's trying to help you."

I got my hands in place on her slim body and pushed. It took about four tries before this big old glob of stuffing came flying out. Looked like it was a little bigger than a golf ball. It hit the floor and then sort of rolled.

Stella coughed hard and took a raggedy deep breath as she sagged against me. I should have dropped her like a sack of potatoes but, I didn't.

I just reacted and grabbed to hold her up. Doing that meant I pretty much cupped her girls, her fun bags, her life-giving sacks, whatever you want to call them. It didn't help that she was braless as she almost always was and she had far more than a cupful. She is built as God blessed her. So, in other words, I had copped a good feel without trying.

She let out a yell that would have made NYPD Police Captain Olivia Benson proud, spun around, and slapped the holy living heck out of me. I staggered back, the whole left side of my face on fire, and put my hands up. She was mad as heck and advanced at me as I tried to explain it was all an accident and I was just trying to help.

Cousin Jimmy decided he had to avenge her besmirched honor. He chose to reward my efforts to help by backing me up against the dining room table and punching me hard in the gut. He hit me low too, just above the jewels, so it hurt worse than it otherwise might have if he had hit me full on, in the stomach. He's always fought dirty, but this wasn't right.

I had a second to think about maybe he was one and done. As I pitched forward, he landed an uppercut that hit me hard in my jaw and took me off my feet. I went head over heels backwards into the dinner table. Laden as it was with so much food, as Leory lays out one heck of a great spread, could not withstand the impact of my three hundred plus additional pounds, too.

Thanksgiving dinner was a bust, literally, and figuratively.

I was still laying on what was left of the table and trying to work out whether mashed potatoes all over my face was helping or hurting me, when I heard sirens and what sounded like at least two squad cars speed in over the gravel out front. Sheriff Block and his boys had arrived. They took a few minutes to survey the scene which allowed Jimmy to run out the back of the house towards the wood line. He might have made it too, if not for what the feral hogs had done a couple of nights earlier. The ground looked like landmines had exploded everywhere. Jimmy, who spent most of the run looking backwards, according to Leroy who had seen him via the kitchen window, put his foot in a hole, and went down hard. As he got up, Marcus, who used to play ball, crashed his bulk into Jimmy and put him back down into the ground. Back in the day, Marcus could tackle and loved nothing more than hitting somebody hard to do it. I figured nailing Jimmy like that might have made his year.

The deputies put the cuffs on and frog-marched Jimmy to the house and though, before shoving him in the back of a patrol car. The Sheriff explained he'd been arrested for stealing a ring from "Big Earl's Pawnshop Emporium" in town. As the Sheriff explained, it seemed like a typical Jimmy stupidity.

Apparently, Cousin Jimmy had been scoping out the ring, and he liked it a lot but, he'd made it clear he thought the $400 price tag was a bit high. So, he and Big Earl had gone back and forth on the price. Big Earl, not only did not like jokes about his under five-foot height, he also did not negotiate prices. It was either pay what he wanted or forget it. Whatever didn't sell in the store, he sold online, and business was apparently good. He didn't negotiate.

Well, Jimmy made it clear he thought $400 was far too much for love and left. Normally, Big Earl would have thought Jimmy was just being Jimmy and all was good. It wasn't the first time they'd argued over a price, but Jimmy always came back, paid the price, and made his purchase. Not this time.

No, not this time. No, Jimmy went around the corner and then came back a few minutes later. The Sheriff explained, as he tried not to laugh, when Jimmy strolled back inside, he had turned his shirt inside out and put a pair of pantyhose over his head. He planned to rob Big Earl and take the ring. Of course, he discovered putting the reinforced crotch part of the pantyhose over his face meant he could not see at all well, so he cut a big old hole in them. He could see as the hole was several inches from top to bottom. Don't know whose pantyhose they were.

Of course, he did not think about how he could be seen by Leroy and the cameras Leroy had everywhere. He came back in and held out his knife, demanded the ring. Leroy never moved to get his double barrel shotgun out from under the counter. Instead, he just gave him the ring. Probably because he was laughing so hard. According to the Sheriff, Jimmy also took a half dozen lottery tickets and a t-shirt that had the Beatles on it.

The same shirt Jimmy was wearing when he showed up and now had grass stains and mud on it. It had been a cool shirt. Now it looked like hell. The was no way Big Earl would take that back, like he could the ring.

The heist of the century had been a little over two hours earlier. The deputies had set up on Jimmy's house, thinking he was at home. No joy there so they had come to Leroy's place. In fact, they would have arrived a good twenty minutes earlier, and my face and jaw would have been way better, if not for them getting stuck at the railroad crossing a few miles down the two-lane road, thanks to the always slow-moving Union Pacific gravel train.

It took forever for the 4 p.m. pass through the area when it was moving. Today it had been stopped a while thanks to one of Wilson's cows that had gotten out, made it over to the tracks, and stubbornly faced off against the train. One of the deputies, new on the force and all gung-ho, decided since Wilson could not get the cow to move, he would shoot it with his non-lethal bean bag rifle.

We were just getting to what had happened to the cow when the Sherriff realized I was sitting on the floor in the remnants of the table and the food. He'd asked me what had happened, but I never got to explain as Stella and Thelma told, occasionally contradictory, versions. When asked, Aunt Thelma pointed out the stuffing ball to the Sheriff who proceeded to walk over and push it around with a black boot. He mushed it this way and that, which did not do a lot for the carpet, but did make the ball of stuffing break up a little. A little more boot poking revealed the ring in a small plastic bag kind of envelope. He bent over and picked it up. He shook the envelope a couple of times and most of the stuffing fell off. He held it up and looked at it for a few seconds, turning it this way and that.

"Yep, that's the ring. Not only did he leave the ring in the little bag Big Earl uses, you can see the price sticker on it," he announced.

Stella had demanded to see it, but the Sheriff had told her no and slipped it into his shirt pocket. Stella tried to argue and then started to cough again.

Sheriff called for the county EMS to come out as he thought she needed to be checked over. Soon the ambulance, which was just a refitted cargo van and not the big city ambulance deal, lights and sirens sounding, came up in the gravel as the squad car with Jimmy rolled away. After Stella got checked and cleared, the Sheriff had me looked at too, as I was feeling a bit dizzy now and then.

Pretty soon I was in the back of the damn thing and taking the ride. The medics had no idea if I had a concussion or not. The hospital folks kept me overnight and then decided I was not concussed and could go home.

Leroy had come to the hospital and brought me back to his place so I could get my car. It was on the drive there, he told me Jimmy apparently pulled the turkey out of the oven, pulled most of the stuffing out, shoved the bagged ring and all into the bird, and packed the stuffing back inside. It explained why Stella had a lot more stuffing than the rest of us and why Jimmy had been so aggressive in handling the dishing out of the plates while Leroy carved the bird.

Neither Jimmy nor Stella ever apologized. Leroy was not mad about the table. He just built a bigger dinner table to replace the broken store-bought one and told me not to worry about it. Everybody seemed to have gone on with their lives, none the worse for wear.

I, on the other hand, was still dealing with it. My stomach was fine. I was pretty sure he'd messed my teeth up because nothing felt right. There was the fact my jaw still hurt now and then when the weather changed.

And stuffing, one of my all-time favorite foods was ruined for me. I could not look at the stuff without my face burning and my jaw aching. I had looked at box stuffing at the store. The idea of eating it made me sick. Just like pumpkin with marshmallows on top, the kind everybody and their dog seem to love, well, just the sight of it made my stomach flip flop like a shed in a hurricane, stuffing was a no go now.

At least, I had not choked on love

Easy Poultry, Rice and Carrot Soup

Combine in a large pot:

4 cups chicken broth

2 cups water

12-16 ounces of cooked chicken or turkey, cut into small pieces-
from a store, leftovers, or canned

¾ cup uncooked minute rice

sprinkles to your taste of whatever is on hand of the following:
marjoram, turmeric, basil, sage, garlic powder, onion powder,
paprika, pepper or cayenne powder, and salt

(1) 14.5 ounce can of sliced carrots, drained

Cover pot with lid. Bring to a boil, then simmer until the rice is
cooked.

What Cranberry Relish Can Add to Your Holiday

Vicki Erwin

Thanksgiving isn't for the faint of heart. It's all about family (feuds), cooking (I hate to cook), and eating (I'm a picky eater).

What I looked forward to on Thanksgiving was the carryout dinner I'd ordered well in advance, reading a little, then hours spent on the streaming series I hadn't had time to watch and was at least two seasons behind. All of this to be accomplished in my pajamas. With a beer. There was a no alcohol rule at my family's gatherings because of Aunt Carol. No one wanted another incident like her the "it's-too-hot-in-here-striptease" of three years ago. That is something none of us can unsee.

My sister Jenna ruined all my plans. My life started its downward spiral when she was born. I'd had a blissful only-child-life up to that moment. After she arrived on the scene, nothing I did measured up to Little Miss Perfect. Or so it seemed.

"Thanksgiving is at my house, *again*." Jenna said with a big sigh when I reluctantly answered the phone. "Be here around eleven."

"I have plans." I removed the phone from my ear in preparation for hanging up.

"No, no, no. This is family. It's required. Besides, we *want* you to come." My sister spoke loudly. She must have known I planned to bail on the call and the holiday.

"Sorry, can't come." Did my sister not remember the family game night we'd had five years ago on this very holiday? It was burned in my memory. I'd won at Trivial Pursuit, Monopoly, and Tripoley (with a cash pot of $162.73). I wasn't a good winner, as I tended to gloat. I wasn't a good loser either, but no one knew because I was a winner, capital "W." Dad had to stop a smackdown with my brother-in-law when I skipped around him, called him loser, and waved the cash I'd won in his face. A neighbor called the police when we moved our disagreement outside. I had to give the money back or be arrested. Gambling is illegal.

"C'mon, Sharon. Don't be like that. You don't have to cook anything."

As if they would ask *me* to cook after the I-forgot-to-refrigerate-the-apple-salad-with mayo-dressing food poisoning incident. I didn't know what would happen so I left it on the counter overnight, so I wouldn't forget to bring it the next day. There was a major plumbing problem resulting from that event. Or, the I-hope-you-have-good-insurance because I watched a revue from a recent Broadway show in the Macy's parade instead of the cooking food and the stove caught on fire. Jenna got a nice new kitchen out of that. We ate at a pizza place we found open. I'm still paying off the charge bill for dinner since it was *all my fault.*

"Mom wants you here," Jenna said. "She has a surprise."

I groaned. She knew Mom was one of my weak spots, although I wasn't at all tempted by the thought of her surprise. Mom's surprises were clothes because she thought I dressed like a prostitute. Or the gift of learning with a class she'd enrolled me in for self-improvement. So far, the improvements included exercise classes, cooking classes, and the absolute worst surprise— signing me up for a dating site. *She wrote my bio.* Some very *interesting* men—and a few women—contacted me because of that fiasco. I preferred to choose my own dates. Or, to not date at all, which was my current status.

"Dennis Junior wants you to come too."

I groaned again. My other soft spot. I adored my nephew. He was the only person in the family I thought accepted me as I was.

"You've poisoned him on the entire idea of Thanksgiving, so you can save him from suffering. Pick up a container of the holiday cranberry relish, the one only available at the Freddie's Market near you. You brought it last year and Dennis loved it. It's one thing Thanksgiving-y he'll eat. Otherwise, it's peanut butter."

The cranberry relish. My one Thanksgiving success with no accompanying disaster. "I did not poison the holiday for Dennis." My nephew joined me in hating the football talk at the table; the ribbing because we wanted to *stick our noses in a book* when there was fun to be had. Overall, the forced family time.

All this sounds like I hate my family. Not true. I need them in small doses, a few at a time, when I choose, and when food is not the prime consideration. I usually mess that part up.

"For Denny and for Mom." I knew I would live to regret it. "I'll come for exactly two hours."

"And bring the cranberry relish."

"Of course."

* * *

As I'm apt to do, I put the thought of Thanksgiving out of my mind as long as possible. The day before—late the evening before—it hit me. The cranberry relish! I checked my watch, 7:15 p.m. I checked online. Freddie's was open for another forty-five minutes.

I pulled into the parking lot at 7:35, give or take, and hurried inside. I should have known from the almost full parking lot it would be crowded. Freddie's wasn't much bigger than my house. I pushed through the crowd to the deli in the back.

"Excuse me, I'd like a quart of your delicious cranberry relish." I called out to the woman behind the counter.

"Take a number."

Dirty looks came at me from the several people lined up along the counter.

I grabbed a number. 7:46 pm.

It took less time than I expected for my number to come up. I asked again for the cranberries. She looked at the skimpy offerings left. "Sorry, all out. There might be a carton or two in the cold case."

I whirled around as a man lifted a small container of something deep red out of the case and headed toward checkout. 7:52 pm.

I reached in for relish and…nothing. Not a single cranberry of any size, shape, or form remained. I needed that relish to save the holiday for me *and* my nephew.

"Sir, sir, excuse me." I grabbed the man's arm, the man who had taken the last carton of relish.

"Well, hello. It's been a while." He turned.

I was speechless—and confused. He was a hunk—aqua eyes, a dark curl curved on the middle of his forehead, and broad shoulders that stretched a t-shirt's cartoon turkey so far it was yelling "Help!"

I swallowed, and as I opened my mouth…

"Five minutes to close. Please make your selections and bring them to checkout." The loudspeaker blared and drowned out my possible reply.

The man gave me a puzzled grin and continued down the aisle.

"No, really. I need…" I grabbed the man's arm again, my hands sweaty. It was 7:58 pm.

He pulled away.

"I need that cranberry relish." I said it so loudly everyone turned toward me. "I really do." I was quieter that time.

"My mom loves the stuff, so I need it, too." He air-quoted "need." He dumped his purchases on the conveyor belt, including *my* relish.

"Please." I wheedled, looked up at him—way up—even fluttered my eyelashes. The things I'd do for cranberry relish.

"Hmph."

I followed him out of the store at 8:01 pm.

"I'll pay double whatever you paid."

He opened the door and folded himself into a small silver sports car.

"No."

I pulled cash out of my purse, waved bills at him. Dennis was my favorite member of my family. I needed those cranberries.

The man started his car and gunned the motor. "I'm leaving now. Please move."

I ran to my car, quickly backed out to follow him. I couldn't give up, not yet.

He drove slowly, given the car looked like it could fly.

Two streets from where I lived, he turned sharply, no signal. Did he just try to lose me? I turned, too.

With no signal again, he swerved into a driveway.

My car screeched as I jerked the steering wheel and…slammed Veronica, my ancient Volvo, into the back of his itsy-bitsy toy car. The crash drove his car—and him—into the wall of his garage.

I may have hit the accelerator instead of the brake when I turned. Nerves, okay?

I sat motionless. No way he'd give me the cranberry relish now. I waited for him to open his car door and stomp toward me, raging mad. It looked like I'd made a mess of his sporty little car. I waited. Was his door stuck?

I stepped out of my car. I crept to the driver's side of his and knocked on the window. He was slumped over the steering wheel, as if too mad to face me. Or too injured? He hadn't been wearing a seat belt. Like Veronica, the car was too old for air bags to cushion an accident.

"So sorry. I have insurance." I knocked again. He still didn't move. The dashboard lights showed viscous red fluid drip along the steering wheel.

With an effort, I pulled open the door and saw a gash along his forehead. And it wasn't cranberry relish that dripped into his lap. I looked around. Where were the neighbors? Couldn't they see I needed help? Weren't there any old people with nothing better to do than stare out their windows and mind other people's business?

I checked for a pulse in his neck and felt a huge sense of relief when it beat strong against my fingers. Thank heaven also for sirens heading our way.

Before I thought better of it, I ran to the other side of the car and grabbed a bag sitting on the seat. I threw it in my car just as emergency vehicles pulled up.

"He's hurt. Must have hit the steering wheel or something." I pointed.

The EMTs went to the driver, checked his pulse. They carefully pulled him out of the car, placed him on a backboard, then the gurney.

His eyes opened and he tried to sit up. The sense of relief was almost enough to bring me to my knees. I hadn't killed him. It lessened my guilt about taking the cranberries. He wouldn't have any need for them. He was likely to spend Thanksgiving in the hospital.

"What happened here?" A female police officer asked, waved a hand toward the crumpled vehicles. "Are you hurt?"

"No, only the driver of that one. I was driving the Volvo." I pointed to Veronica, admitted guilt that caused the injury to the poor man who only tried to buy his mom Thanksgiving cranberry relish. It was okay. She'd be at the hospital with her son.

"It's a driveway," the officer said.

I shrugged. My insurance company would throw a major fit and probably cancel my coverage. The least that would happen would be a hefty increase in premium.

The officer took cell phone pictures of my car, his car, and the glass on the ground from both.

I walked to where the EMTs examined the man.

"What's his name?" A cute EMT with a sparse mustache asked me.

I shook my head. "No idea."

The police officer interrupted the EMT before he asked more questions I couldn't answer. She led me to her car, and her questions were much easier—my name, address, to see my license and insurance. Then she, too, asked the injured man's name.

"I don't know."

"How did this happen?"

"Maybe my foot slipped?"

"But you're in his *driveway*."

I cleared my throat. "He had something of mine. I needed it." It was mine, now. Possession is nine-tenths of the law, right?

Before she could proceed, a tow truck pulled up. The driver got out and slid into my Volvo.

"Hey, wait a minute!" The police officer held me back. "What's he doing to my car?"

"That car isn't drivable," she said.

The tow driver tried to start the engine several times to no avail. My heart sank. Veronica had been our car, mine and the parents, for years. I'd driven it to college and ever since. Mainly because I couldn't afford anything else. I loved her despite her age. Was this the death of Veronica?

The EMTs rolled the cranberry thief (or was that me?) past us. I'd swear he opened his eyes long enough to give me a poisonous look before he was shoved in the back of the ambulance and driven away, siren blaring. By then, neighbors had come outside and formed a viewing audience.

The tow truck driver stuck a horrible-looking hook in Veronica's private parts. It gave me shivers to just think about it. Tears burned my eyes as she left, dragging behind the tow truck. A second tow truck drove up behind the silver sports car and poof! It, too, was gone.

Then it hit me. My cranberry relish was in the Volvo's back seat.

The police officer left me unsupervised while she talked to a few people in the crowd. As she finally walked toward me, a voice came over the radio she wore on her shoulder.

"Do you have a way home?" she called as she ran to her car and opened the door.

I nodded. I lived two blocks away, an easy walk. Yet I'd somehow missed this man among men who lived so close. Maybe that's why he'd spoken to me as if he knew me. "Where are they taking my car?"

The officer yelled words I didn't understand as she raced away, her siren blaring.

"Are you okay, miss?" An older man stepped toward me as the crowd, bit of a misnomer for the six people gathered, dispersed.

"They took my car. It had a vital Thanksgiving element in the back seat."

"It'll be at the police impound," he said. "You know where that is?"

"Of course, I don't know where it is!" Did I look like I knew the inner working of the police? I was a little testy by then.

"1127 Boulevard," he said. "Used to be an arm of the law myself. Worked security at the mall for 29 years."

Sure. "Thank you for that info." I tried to sound grateful. It wouldn't hurt to practice a little for Thanksgiving.

I walked home. It was surprisingly warm for November in Missouri. I hoped it turned to rain before the next afternoon or the men, any male, no matter age or fitness, in the family would insist on playing football. Did they think we were the Kennedys?

What to do about Dennis' cranberry relish? I'd rescue it. I ran next door and asked Barry, my good-hearted neighbor, if I could borrow his car.

"Been in any accidents lately?" He laughed.

"Umm, no, of course not." I laughed, not as heartily.

He picked the keys off a hook beside his door and threw them to me. I missed and had to feel along the side of the porch in the dark and dirt to find them.

"You're responsible for any damage, little girl." He laughed again. Or maybe still.

"You bet!" I ran to his car and, since I wasn't a very good stick shift driver, screeched and bucked out of the drive. He stopped laughing.

As I drove, I entered the address of the impound in my phone's GPS. The lot wasn't far. On arrival, I was faced with a locked gate and closed sign.

WE WILL REPOPEN FRIDAY, NOVEMBER 21 AT 8 AM.
HAPPY THANKSGIVING.

Not without that cranberry relish, it won't be!

I peered through the wire fence at the lot. There was my poor Veronica. Next to her was the sports car. I hoped it wasn't giving her too hard a time. Imagining a conversation between two cars, not to mention how the hook felt up my car's backside, made me wonder if I spent too much time alone.

I walked along the fence to check for a place with no barbed wire across the top. I wasn't there to take a car. All I was doing was removing what belonged to me—sort of. It would do me no good on Friday morning.

There was a second gate at the back, perhaps for workers. I could easily climb over it, especially since there was no barbed wire. I made it to the top, then threw my leg over. The seam along the rear of my pants ripped and exposed parts that are best left covered. As I slid to the ground, the edge of my slacks caught on an errant wire and ripped further, leaving my now chilled backside in full view. Once on the ground, I tried to tuck in the torn part to cover my parts as best I could.

The good news was Veronica's locks no longer worked, something to do with child locks. Since I had no children, it had never been a problem. It was a moment to be grateful for, not taking care of routine maintenance on my car.

I removed the bag with the relish and checked to make sure the tow truck driver hadn't helped himself. I gasped. There was no cranberry relish! For about the fifteenth time that evening, my stomach sank. Did I miss a second bag. I moved to the silver car.

Luck was with me for a change. Not only was there another Freddie's bag, the window had broken when I hit the car. I stuck my arm inside and grabbed the relish.

My arm was still there when lights flashed and sirens blared throughout the lot. A police car slid to a stop in front of the gate. A second car pulled up more slowly and parked beside it. My arm remained inside the car that wasn't mine.

The man from the second car unlocked the gate for the same female police officer who had been at the accident. She had her hand on her gun as she walked toward me.

"You again?" she said.

"It's me. Sharon Carnegie." I ho-hoed.

The police officer was not amused. "I thought you were driving the Volvo?"

"I was."

"Why is your arm inside Mr. Herring's car?"

I pulled my arm out, clutching the bag. Herring? The name rang a distant bell.

"Thought he might need this." I giggled again, nervous, held up the bag. The shape was right for the container of cranberry relish.

"You didn't even know his name at the scene," the officer said.

"I was upset?"

"Hand over the bag."

My precious cranberry relish. I didn't want to. I couldn't. But I did.

"It's food," she said.

"Hospital food is the worst," I said.

"Did you hit your head? When the cars collided?"

The man who had unlocked the gate stepped up. "How did you get in here?"

I turned around and let my torn pants do the talking. When I turned back, the man was as red as the cranberries. The police officer had covered her mouth. I was pretty sure she was trying not to laugh.

"The cranberry relish is for my nephew. For Thanksgiving," I said.

The officer said nothing.

Our friend with the keys had returned to the gate, where he pulled out his phone.

"Could you wait until Friday to arrest me? I'll come into the station on my own, and you can take care of whatever, then?" It wouldn't hurt to ask.

She chewed on her lower lip. "Only because it's a holiday; it's late; and I want to spend time with my family at my house. Not the station. Remember, I know where you live." She shook her finger at me.

"I'll be there," I promised. "Will I have to go to jail?" I didn't think a car accident, especially since I had insurance, would be enough to land me in the hoosegow. Breaking into the police impound? I should have thought that through. Of course, there were cameras and alarms.

She sighed. "Don't get into any more trouble before then."

I held up three fingers in a Scout's promise and hoped spending an afternoon with my family wouldn't make me break my vow.

* * *

I barely slept, partly because I was sore from the crash, but mostly because I worried about Mr. Herring. My thoughts ranged from he's just fine to what if he has traumatic brain injury or died. The only way to rid myself of the worry was to see the man for myself. Fortunately, I still had Barry's car.

I assumed the ambulance would take him to the nearest hospital, especially since it didn't seem he was talking much after the accident. I headed to St. Joseph's.

When I arrived, the volunteer (on Thanksgiving?) told me he was still in the emergency department where no visitors were allowed but it didn't stop me. I followed the arrows and almost caused another Herring-Carnegie collision when he burst out of the swinging doors of the ER.

"You!" He had bandages around his head and wrist. He remembered me, so he couldn't be too badly injured.

"Hi," was all I could think of to say.

We stared at one another. He looked damn good for someone who had been in a car wreck only a few hours earlier.

After a stuttering start, I said, "I wanted to make sure you were alright."

"Good as new." He pointed at the head bandage with his hand bandage.

"My mom would say, 'Hope that knocked some sense in you.'"

From his frown, Mr. Herring didn't think my mom was funny.

"I have insurance and it'll take care of all the bills. Your car's at police impound. I'll take you home, if you don't have a wife, mother, or friend available."

Could they please stitch my mouth closed? Why did I offer to take him home?

"You don't remember me, do you?"

"The accident was last night. I didn't hit my head. Of course I remember." Maybe he did have damage.

"From school. We graduated from the same high school. The same year."

Whaa-at? I looked him over again. "Did you play football?"

"I hadn't had my growth spurt yet," he said.

He was trying not to grin. Herring. Herring. Oh! Jason Herring, a short, skinny dude, with glasses and very cropped hair, no curls. His pants were always clown pants big and usually too short.

"Jason?"

He nodded and crossed his arms over a chest that was wider than two of high school Jason's. He'd worked out during his growth spurt.

"I guess that's one more thing to be sorry for, not recognizing you, along with hurting you, and destroying your car."

"My car is destroyed?" For the first time, he showed panic.

"I don't know. Really. I said that because it was towed. It's crumpled and the windows are damaged. You can check tomorrow. The lot is closed today."

"My mom's cranberries are ruined." He grinned for sure this time.

"I … rescued them. I mean, I didn't want them to go to waste." My face grew hot, then hotter.

"You can have them. We aren't having Thanksgiving until Sunday. They'll make more before then," Jason said.

"Why wouldn't you give them to me last night?" I was slightly put out. This situation could have been avoided.

"I wish I had All I could think about was, you didn't recognize me."

Did he realize how ridiculous it was to hold a grudge for so long?

"And with our history." He smiled a flirty smile. My stomach fluttered.

Time to change the subject. "How about I drop off the relish later today?" I needed to get away. He was giving me all the feels.

"How about we stop by your house and pick it up when you spring me from this hospital?" he said.

"You need a ride?"

"Mom doesn't drive. My brothers are at their in-laws; coming in this weekend with the grandkids so we can kick off the holiday season together," Jason said.

No wife or girlfriend either, it appeared. "Sure, sure. Where's your stuff?"

"I came in with the clothes on my back," he said. "They cut those off to fix my shoulder." He rubbed it and made a face. "It was dislocated."

Great. Another injury to feel bad about.

"Explains why I am wearing this shirt." Jason tapped the big heart with "I love my nurse" written inside it. "I did not love my nurse. She was far too handy with a needle."

"Come to my family's Thanksgiving," I said, then clapped my hand over my mouth.

He stared down at me. Jason had grown at least a foot since our school days.

"You don't mean that. I bought a turkey pot pie for my dinner. Except it was in my car when you destroyed it." Jason grinned again, like the accident was a big joke. *I* still had to face the police about it.

I had that turkey pot pie. It had been in the first bag I took from his car.

"Unacceptable," I said. "We'll stop by your house, and you can change, then we'll pick up the cranberry relish for my nephew. He's a challenging eater. If I don't bring this one thing, he'll only eat peanut butter for Thanksgiving. That's why I wanted it so badly."

"I understand. One of my nieces only eats noodles."

"What's with these kids?" I said. I held the door open and led Jason to the car.

"Good thing you have an extra car." He buckled his seat belt.

"It's my neighbor's." I backed out, the car only bucking slightly as I changed gears.

"Does he know ..."

"He doesn't. So don't say anything or we'll be walking to my sister's house."

"He'll know something is up when they cart you off to jail."

"Don't tease about that. I have to show up at the police station on Friday."

Jason wasn't faking his surprise. "But I'm not pressing charges. For the accident or for the theft of my cranberry relish."

"I broke into the police impound lot to find the relish. The first bag I grabbed from your car was the turkey pot pie."

Jason laughed, hard. He didn't stop until I pulled into his driveway. I stopped properly this time.

"I'm an attorney. I'll defend you. Let me grab a clean shirt and brush my teeth. Be right back."

He was an attorney. And single. We had a history and he remembered me. I continued to indulge in daydreams about Jason until he returned.

At my house, I ran inside and picked up the cranberry relish. I also grabbed the turkey pie.

Jenna's mouth practically hit the floor when she opened the door. "Jason Herring? Is that you?" she said, making me feel worse for not recognizing him.

"Living and breathing, sort of."

Oops, I hadn't said anything to him about not mentioning how we'd reconnected.

"Looks like an ow-ee on your head," my sister said.

"Twelve stitches."

Jenna looked at me. If she'd been a cartoon, there would be question marks in her eyes.

"Is it okay for Jason to join us?" I said. "He brought his own dinner." I handed her the turkey pie.

My sister cleared her throat as she stared at it. "Th-thanks?"

Jason elbowed me. He was only slightly amused.

Mom joined us. "Jason, it's been a long time. You've certainly grown up well!"

Mom recognized him?

"Thanks for inviting me, Mrs. Carnegie."

Inviting him?

"I thought it was time for you and Sharon to reconnect. When you were little, you loved to play together. I brought a couple of snapshots of the two of you." Mom motioned for us to follow her.

Son of a b…gun. This must have been Mom's surprise.

In the vein of Thanksgiving events I wish had never happened, Mom brought out a series of photos from when we were very young.

"These are from when Jason's family lived down the street from us. If I'm not mistaken, he was your first kiss. He moved away and went to a different elementary and middle school. You were back together in high school, right?"

I blushed. My first kiss? There was a vague memory in the back of my mind of a swing set and a peck on the lips.

"Different crowd by then," Jason said.

"I like this one." Mom held up a black and white snapshot of me holding a hose and spraying Jason. Neither one of us wore anything but white underpants.

I grabbed for it, but Jason got it first.

"Mom, how could you let me out without clothes, and why did you take a picture of it?" The heat of embarrassment went all the way to my toes.

"I didn't 'let' you. You took off your clothes all the time. I had to keep a close eye to make sure you kept those undies on." Mom shook her head. "You were a handful."

"I think she convinced me to take mine off by saying I'd be in trouble if I went home in wet clothes, and then she sprayed me with the hose." Mom and Jason shared a laugh.

"Come help me, Sharon!" Jenna called.

"Don't let her near the stove!" Mom was less than supportive.

Surely, she wouldn't give Jason a rundown of all the Thanksgivings I'd ruined.

Jenna had me set the table, which I managed without mishap, and soon everyone sat down to eat.

Dennis had been happy to see me. And he inhaled the cranberry relish.

I kept a close eye on the time. I'd said two hours, but it turned out to be almost three by the time we ate and cleaned up. Jason was trying to explain why he couldn't play football when I told him we had to go.

"Sure." He shook hands with everyone and gave Mom a hug. There was a chorus of stay awhile! Don't go! All directed at Jason.

"If you want to stay, I'm sure someone will take you home later." I'd barely spoken to Jason since we'd arrived; he was a big hit with the family.

"I'll go with you."

Jason didn't spill the tea about either the car accident or my possible incarceration. I let out a long sigh in the car.

"Nice family," Jason said, waving at them as we drove away.

"Thanks for putting up with them."

"I loved it. If you want, you can come to my family Thanksgiving on Sunday."

My stomach fluttered again. I looked at him to make sure he meant it. He looked like…

"Stop! Stop!" Jason yelled.

I slammed on the brakes and the car engine died as we stopped in the middle of the intersection, barely missing a BMW. I should have watched the road, not the man beside me. And that the traffic light was red.

"I'll drive Sunday." Jason rubbed a hand over his face.

"I'll bring the cranberry relish."

And that's when he kissed me. Damn if he didn't taste like cranberry relish.

A Faery Tale Thanksgiving
Fedora Amis

Few people have sympathy for the cash flow problems of professional criminals. Well, let me tell you, the worry just about takes the fun out of a speedy getaway or a perfect mugging.

So that's why the story I'm about to tell is particularly sad. In fact, I'm shedding tears this very minute.

Here's how desperate my partner and I became because of the high cost of living for people like us who are reduced to wearing second-hand hoodies and cheap sunglasses. The upkeep on heist equipment is somewhere between poisonous and impossible. Cars, for one. I've never been more embarrassed than the time I had to ask an Uber driver to speed up because the cops were gaining on us.

Groceries are so pricey we must eat every meal at a greasy-spoon diner. Don't get me started on rent. We're forced to live in a motel with highway traffic rattling the windows. Most rooms rent by the hour, but our stay is semi-permanent because the TV is broke. Surprising that the TV matters. The walls are thin as plastic wrap, though you can't see through unless you poke a hole.

With a set-up like that, Rodney would go psychedelic if he didn't break at least a few rules. Tearing up a pillow with his teeth or kicking out a door slat calms him down—sometimes for a whole hour.

Breaking the HD-TV in half was the best idea Rodney ever had. In fact, it was the only decent idea he ever had. When the manager offered to supply a new widescreen, Rodney vetoed the notion. With one hand to the back of the manager's shirt collar and the other to the seat of his pants, Rodney tossed the yokel out into the parking lot. I held the door.

From that day on, the manager was quite content to comp us the room. After all, we had no TV.

The upshot is we had no choice but to entertain ourselves. Our minds naturally turned to making money. We could ply our usual ploys like snatch a purse or two. That was our best day job. At night we could do a break and grab in a jewelry store window or stand on a pool hall parking lot until the winner comes out. We'd tried all sorts of ways. Frankly, each one had its own drawbacks.

Think about it. Purses and wallets don't carry real money anymore— just credit cards. We could sell those doofy bits of plastic, but the buyers don't want to pay cash. They want to transfer money into our bank account—which we don't have. Well, we did have one, but that was before Rodney robbed the branch where we did business.

Our last brick thrown at a jewelry store glass window bounced off and smacked Rodney in the eye. He became so depressed that for days he moped around in his boxers swilling brews—until the beer ran out. Turned out OK though. Being beerless nudged him back to work.

But the pool hall disaster was the worst of all—at least for me. The winner was a woman, so Rodney said I should do the stickup—my first ever. Turns out, she broke my jaw with her elbow, shoved me down on the asphalt, and damn near cut my throat with a bobby pin. When Rodney stepped in, she used the hairpin on him—made a big gash on the side of his face. He's been letting his beard grow to cover it.

We got desperate enough to try bankruptcy, but the lawyer said only people who had money and paid taxes could apply.

All this is by way of proving the Bonnie-and-Clyde lifestyle may be glamorous but is a financial troll under a bridge.

Take for example, the doctor who set my jaw and tended Rodney's scrapes and scratches. He wanted to charge us enough to buy a cow. Cows cost $3,000.00. I looked it up. But we lacked the beans even for that. The manager threatened to turn us in to the cops. We couldn't go that route because we were wanted for murder. We didn't do it, I swear.

But if the authorities can fry you and clear their books, you can bet your silver skates and best bikini they will.

That's when the doc came up with a new plan. It seemed foolproof. Snatch the only daughter of a rich guy, trade her for half a million—no need to be greedy—and retire to Madagascar.

The good doctor told me all I needed to know. Where they lived, which room the girl slept in, and where to set the exchange. He even supplied surgical gloves so no fingerprints. Chloroform, too, to get around any shenanigans she might try. Of course, we'd have to raise the ransom to three-quarters of a million and give him a third.

Back at the motel, Rodney said we should ask for a whole million—a nice, round number. I tried to wise him up. Told him we'd have to give a third to the doctor, and I didn't know how to divide a million into three equal parts.

Rodney said, "Never mind. We're not giving the doctor a third. In fact, no cut at all."

There goes Rodney—trying to think again.

I explained as best I could. "I don't want to charge old Frick too awful much. He might think his girl is not worth the dough. Besides, if this caper goes well, we could come back later and make a higher bid in round two." Rodney smiled at that and let me set the price.

I must say, the plan looked a treat—much easier than following a FedEx truck and swiping porch parcels. Half the time you end up with trash you don't even know what it is. But grabbing a rich girl would be perfect. In and out, no fingerprints, back to the motel in time for breakfast.

Next morning, I shinnied up an apple tree and bounded over the balcony rail faster than a hoppin' hare. Credit card to the lock on the French doors—at least that sorry plastic is good for something. Then inside without so much as tripping the alarm.

As I stood there waiting for my eyes to adjust, I stared at the girl in her bed. I should have kept my mind on estimating her size and heft, but with her golden hair spread out on her pillow, she looked like

Sleeping Beauty in the fairy tale. I hate to admit it, but she hypnotized me.

All of a sudden, she sat bolt upright and said, "Hilaria, turn on all the lights." Next thing I knew, the room was more lit up than twenty drunks on New Year's Eve. I know about Alexa and Siri, but I never heard of Hilaria. Must be for millionaires only. The name sounded funny. I didn't laugh, though. Kept my cool.

The blaze of light nearly blinded me. I opened my eyes to wonders beyond belief. I never saw any place half so grand as that bedroom. The furniture was all white with gold curlicues. But compared to that bed, all the other pieces belonged in the trash heap. I swear the bed was a dead ringer for the golden coach in Cinderella, right down to the pumpkin-colored satin bedspread and sparkly green crown on top.

I finally remembered my rubber gloves, but I didn't get them on quite right. I took so long, I was sure she'd find a gun and shoot me or at least start screaming, but she didn't.

When I tried to unscrew the cap from the chloroform, my hands got all twisted up in the gloves.

Cool as a cube, she asked, "Who are you and what are you doing here?"

Shocked me so bad, I spilled chloroform all over the bed.

She hustled out the other side of the bed and repeated herself.

I said, "I'm going to kidnap you. That's all you need to know."

"Kidnap me? You must think—" She cut her own self off, then started up again as though she entertained criminals in her bedroom every Thursday morning. "I've never been kidnapped before. How can I help?"

She surprised me more than I surprised her. "You want to help? Why?"

She bent over to put on her slippers. "Big Stick Frick. He takes me for granted, and I'm tired of it. You know why they call him Big Stick, don't you?"

Naturally, I did, but she didn't seem to. I decided to be cagey. "Got no idea. How'd he get that moniker?"

"He speaks softly and carries a big stick like Theodore Roosevelt. Frick's stick is made of money."

Yeah, right. "I never heard of Theodore Roosevelt. What's it got to do with you wanting to help me kidnap you, anyways?"

"You can help me teach Big Stick a lesson—and take him for a pile of money besides." She stretched her arm across the bed and stuck out her hand for me to shake.

I may be a newcomer to kidnapping, but I'm no fool. When I leaned toward her, I got fumes of chloroform up my nose and my head began to spin. I backed away and took a few swallows of outside air. It dawned on me she *planned* for me to get woozy. "I'm onto you, Miss Frick. Don't you try no more tricks on me."

She came around the bed and held out her wrists. "For handcuffs, but you really don't need them. I'm perfectly content to come without manacles."

Good thing too. I didn't think to bring big twistie ties. I trusted the chloroform, but it was all spilled.

When I took her hand and started to leave, she tilted her head. "Aren't you forgetting something?"

"What?"

"The note. Shouldn't you leave a ransom note?"

"Doc didn't say to leave no note."

"How is anyone supposed to know I'm gone?"

"Missing clothes."

"I have lots of clothes. No one takes inventory of my closets."

"Put some on, then."

"Better to wear my nightie. It will make the kidnapping look more real." She held out her flimsy skirts to show me. "Powder blue chiffon. Do you like it?"

"Better put on more than that. November gets cold."

"I can use this." She pulled the cover off the bed and draped it around her shoulders. "There. I feel like a princess with a golden train."

Miss Frick swished to a desk and returned with a diary and a pen which she gave to me.

After a minute or two, I said, "I don't know what to say."

"Would you like me to dictate?"

I nodded.

"We have abducted—that's A-B-D-U-C-T-E-D your daughter. Put a million dollars in small bills in a tote bag and place it…"

Guess we're demanding a whole million. We can tell Doc it's only three-quarters. Then it occurred to me she was waiting for me to name the drop site. I wrote "Turtle Park" and tossed the diary on the bed. She made sure it stayed open to the right page.

I motioned for her to go outside. On the balcony, I threw one leg over the railing and held a hand out to her.

"Surely you don't expect me to jump off the balcony. I could break a leg. I doubt Big Stick Frick would pay top dollar if you damage the merchandise." She spotted Rodney glaring up at us. "Have your man go to the garden shed and bring back a ladder. The shed is always unlocked. I'm amazed you didn't know."

I was not happy to discover I could have used a ladder instead of climbing an apple tree and hurling myself onto a balcony. Rodney was not happy about fetching a ladder, but he did it. Unfortunately, he didn't wear his rubber gloves. Even little mistakes like that can come back to haunt you. That's another reason why a life of crime has more than its share of drawbacks.

The sound of far off police sirens lit a fire under me. In short order we were down the ladder and off to the motel in an Uber driven by a man who asked question after question. I'll admit we made an odd threesome. Not many people ride Ubers at 5:30 a.m.

I was kinda glad Miss Frick fielded most of the questions herself. I didn't know how to answer his first one, "What are you three doing up so early?"

Without thinking for even one second, Miss Frick saved my bacon.

"Good sir, you are in error. We are not rising to meet the new day.

We have just finished a night of revelry at the Frick mansion—a masquerade ball. The master of the manor always throws a fancy dress party on the evening before Thanksgiving." She leaned toward the driver. "Don't you think our costumes are splendid?"

"Yeah, you bet. But what are you supposed to be?"

"Can't you tell? Strongman, cat burglar, and princess. I apologize you can't identify me as a princess. I seem to have lost my tiara. The party got a little raucous. The strongman lost his leopard skin loincloth, too."

"Yes, leopard skin and tiara would make all the difference. The cat burglar is perfect, though."

He asked more stuff, but I didn't pay attention. I was too busy drooling over the idea of Rodney in a leopard skin loincloth—and nothing else.

No sooner did we get back to the motel than Miss Frick started in on us about Thanksgiving. Did we have mashed potatoes or sweet? Stuffing inside the turkey or baked separate? When she demanded fresh cranberry relish instead of the canned stuff, I stopped her cold. "We'll have Jack-in-the-Box burgers. And that's all there is to that."

Miss Frick teared up and reached a hand toward Rodney. He gave her his handkerchief but didn't let her keep it. He needed it for the tears dripping down his beard onto his shirt.

He didn't have to say it. We needed a proper Thanksgiving dinner. I scrounged a bit of newspaper from the wastebasket and started a list. "This is a holiday. I don't think anything will be open, but I'll try. I'm willing to *try* but look around you. We got no table. Where would we put dinner?"

"It's a lovely fall day. Why don't we eat outside by the pool?" Miss Frick had a snappy answer for everything.

I was ahead of her. "Got deck chairs but no table."

"When we came in, I saw some pieces of plywood."

"Four foot by eight foot. Nowhere to put that up as a table except in the road or in the swimming pool."

"Perfect. I've never eaten a meal in an empty swimming pool. We can use my coverlet as a tablecloth." Miss Frick batted her eyes at Rodney. "Perhaps the gentleman here will be kind enough to arrange chairs and table while you get the food. The Church of the Blessed Eggplant sells big pans of meatless turkey and vegetarian side dishes. It's only two blocks away. This is their biggest fundraiser of the year."

"How am I supposed to carry all that?"

"I'll come along if you'll loan me something to wear."

Besides the basics, we returned loaded down with rolls, containers of peas, corn casserole, celery stuffed with peanut butter, and cranberry sauce—not fresh—in a can.

Halfway back, she stopped so short that I ran into a mailbox. "We forgot the whipped topping for the pumpkin pie." She set her pans down on the sidewalk. "Be back in a jiffy." She held out her hand "I'll need money, though. Next time you kidnap a lady remind her to bring her purse."

"Oh, no you don't. I'm not letting you out of my sight. I told you once already. No tricks. Don't try for a third one or you'll be sorry." I watched her pick up her food cartons. "Pie is just as tasty without." Okay, So I lied about the pie. No way would I let her get away with getting away.

Well, smack me in the face with an ugly duck. I was in for another big surprise—a bigger surprise than Miss Frick's good cheer and helpfulness. When we reached the motel, the Thanksgiving table looked downright festive. True, it was in an empty swimming pool, but that made it somehow more charming than an old fuddy-duddy regular table in a dining room or kitchen.

The bedspread turned a slab of plywood into a table fit for royalty and a traditional Thanksgiving feast.

What's more, we had a full complement of strangers and neighbors. I got to admit the manager rose to the occasion. He must have invited every Tom and Tootsie in the joint. He helped, too. For ambiance, whatever that is, he brought along his whole store of if-the-electricity-goes-off candles. The cornucopia of painted fruit from the check-in desk made a handsome centerpiece.

Various others brought holiday spirit—and spirits—lots of the kind that comes in brown bottles. One fellow brought his banjo. No one could think of a proper song to celebrate Thanksgiving, but he knew "Turkey in the Straw," so he played that.

I counted three mismatched-in-age couples including two good-looking lesbians. A sweet couple from Guatemala had six children who fought non-stop over a soccer ball. Thank heavens the children spoke some English. Miss Frick ordered the brats to give her the soccer ball, but they wouldn't do it. She tried to make the papa take the ball away, but I guess her Spanish wasn't up to par. She said he was too soft to be a dad.

By my second piece of pumpkin pie, I was mellow Jello. I must have nodded off. When I woke up, I panicked. All three couples had vanished. The liquor, too. Miss Frick was gone, and the soccer ball was nowhere in sight. "Where is she? Where's the lady?"

Wearing a dopey-drunk look on his face, the manager said, "Ask your Rodney friend, down at the other end of the table. The two of them talked a while, then he gave her all the money in his wallet, and she took off."

I was too poleaxed to say a word. I wasn't the only one not talking. The Guatemalan parents had their heads down on the table. Their brats had all climbed up on the bedspread and were taking a *siesta*—on the exact spot where the chloroform spilled.

I finally managed to spit out a few words. "Rodney wanted to get money *from* her. Why would he give money *to* her?"

The manager shrugged his shoulders. "Not my business. For all I know, those two might be married. I'm wrong about lots of stuff. I thought you and Rodney were homos."

I yelled at the manager. "Get out of my way."

I didn't bother to go around the table. I leaped right up on top and half ran, half crawled my way down the plywood and over the sleeping

Guatemalans. Horn of Plenty became Horn of Empty when fake fruit went flying out both sides.

At the far end of the table, Rodney sat nursing a highball glass and smiling like Old King Cole. I grabbed him by his shirt collar and shook him. "How could you let her go? We got out of bed in the middle of the night. We spent all our money on food for this meal to please her. All except the hundred we keep for a true emergency. The manager tells me you gave her that, too. And now, Doc is gonna kill us Tell me one good reason why I shouldn't choke you to death right here, right now."

Rodney pushed my arm away from his collar and pulled a scribbled-on diary page out of his shirt pocket.

I snatched the paper and read, "I've never had a more enjoyable day in my entire life. I thank you from the bottom of my heart for an unforgettable Thanksgiving."

P.S. My name is Prevaricator Mendacity. I'm glad you made a wrong turn at the mansion.

P.P.S. You should see Miss Frick's room sometime. It's unbelievably magnificent—like something straight out of Cinderella.

The Turducken Murder

Lisa Krystosek

"Pumpkin Spice." Lorna laced her fingers around the latte. "That's the true victim."

"Flavor bullies?" I asked.

"No doubt. Lavender wants the heat off itself. It's in cahoots with Salted Caramel."

"Seasonal fare shouldn't have to suffer such abuse." I crawled into the passenger seat, careful not to spill.

Lorna inhaled the warm steam of her drink. "The sweet smell of a stereotype."

"Do I fit that stereotype?"

"Well," Lorna considered. "You are blonde." She took a sip and grinned. "But the spiky pink highlights make it a solid no."

"I still think pumpkins get a raw deal. They're not even involved in the whole spice controversy. Total scapegourds."

"Worse than goats?"

"Oh yeah," I scoffed. "Goats will chow down on some pumpkin. Scapegourds have it much worse."

"You're the most ridiculous person in this car."

We laughed because it was true. Lorna shifted into drive.

Return to the route.

"We needed coffee," Lorna explained to the navigation screen. "GPS lady is so testy."

"She knows what you ordered."

* * *

Mom calling.

Lorna pressed a button on the steering wheel. "Hey Mom, we'll be there in thirty."

"Wonderful, dear." The disembodied voice of Margo Harvester flowed through the speakers. "Dad put your Reenactment costume in your closet."

My head whipped toward Lorna. She looked horrified.

"I'm not doing it this year."

"You don't mean that." Her mother dismissed the comment.

"Mom, I told you both…"

"Margo, we have a situation." A male voice interrupted.

Lorna's lips pressed into a thin line. She flipped the blinker and sped past a cautious driver.

"What is it, dear?" Margo responded.

"We have a turkey down in the front yard."

My eyes widened. Lorna blasted by three more cars.

"I have to go help your father," Margo said. "See you soon. Can't wait to meet Al."

Call ended.

A few beats went by and Lorna glanced at me. "Inflatables."

"A blow-up turkey?"

"Pilgrims and pumpkins too." She sighed heavily. "And a giant cornucopia."

"A horn of plenty?"

"They're obsessed with holiday yard decor."

My mind shifted gears. "They know I'm female, right?" I asked for the millionth time.

"Yes, *Alice*." Lorna patted my arm.

Hardly anyone called me Alice. It's mostly Al or Als. My name can be a source of confusion and my relationship with Lorna is too important to risk a misunderstanding.

"My parents are fine," Lorna assured me. "Joey's a problem, but you know that."

Joey, Lorna's younger brother, is a train wreck. When his name comes up in conversation, it's in the form of a grievance. My psych degree suspects he's got a touch of the narcissism.

"It's only a couple of days," Lorna said. "What's the worst that can happen?"

* * *

Mulberry Grove could win the charming award. The perfect backdrop for all those cheesy romcoms I secretly adored. About a mile outside of town, Lorna pointed to a rustic sign enshrined in the glow of the setting sun.

"Pinewood Acres. My OG hood."

It's a fairy tale. Cozy bungalows nestled amongst the trees. Friendly neighbors wave from porches. Maybe this Thanksgiving will be different. A strange flickering crushed my hopes. Fairy tales always have a dark side.

"Patriotic light show?" I asked.

Elmhurst Lane was packed with law enforcement vehicles ablaze with flashing lights. An officer blocked our progress and approached the driver's side.

"State your business." The officer swept the beam of his flashlight through the vehicle. He eyed the forgotten lattes with suspicion.

"I'm Lorna Harvester. My parents live at 1010 Elmhurst."

"You are?" The officer's flashlight blinded me.

"She's my girlfriend, Alice," Lorna answered.

The light remained in my face.

"Full name?"

"Like she said, I'm Alice. Do you need my license? Passport? Birth certificate?" I verbally vomited anxiety. "Last name G-A-R-A-M-O-N-D." Heat flushed my cheeks. "You know, like the font?"

"No, Ma'am." The officer shut me down. He swung the flashlight toward the curb. "Park the vehicle over there."

Lorna complied. We exited the car without comment. I was acutely aware of the officer's assessing eyes as we pulled our bags out of the trunk. He ushered us down the sidewalk toward the commotion. An ambulance rolled by and lined up behind a firetruck parked in front of a crowded yard. A woman noticed us. Dark wavy hair skimmed her shoulders. She wrapped a long cardigan around her tall frame, in a familiar posture, an older version of Lorna.

"Prepare yourself." Lorna whispered as her mother made her way across the lawn. "She's an aggressive hugger."

Margo targeted Lorna first, grasped her tightly. Without a word, she released her daughter and pulled me in for the perfect hug.

"All this because someone popped Dad's turkey?" Lorna swept her arms toward the chaos.

"Not exactly, dear."

Margo masked her worry with a smile and hooked an arm through Lorna's. She mirrored the action with me and steered us toward the mayhem. Colossal pilgrims loomed over the unfolding scene. Air-filled pumpkins dotted the yard as a gigantic cornucopia spilled its bounty toward a nearby police huddle. An officer called to Margo.

"Forensics arrived." The officer brightened at the sight of Lorna. "Hey there, stranger."

"Hi, Sheriff Winkle," Lorna said with genuine affection.

"You must be Alice." The sheriff smiled at me.

"Guilty as charged," I joked, then panicked. "I mean, I didn't do anything. We just got here."

"Sheriff?" A voice from the huddle rescued me from myself.

* * *

My curiosity followed the sheriff to a colorful tarp on the ground. The deflated turkey. He lifted a nylon wing.

"That's a person!" Lorna shouted.

I leaned in to get a better look. Sure enough, there was a human under the fabric. I stepped closer. Male. Lying on his right side, arms behind his back, wrists and ankles bound in grey duct tape. His knees pulled up underneath his chin. Tape wrapped around his legs and body to secure the tucked position. Dark splotches mottled his white shirt.

Not moving.

Lorna clung to her mother while I edged closer to the gruesome scene. An empty pumpkin pie box was taped to the body. *Ungrateful Bastard* scrawled across the clear plastic top. I was torn between disgust and fascination.

"It's Tom Henn," Margo cried. "My boss."

Lorna comforted her mother. I should do the same, but my inner comedian invaded my brain. Instead of expressing sympathy, I snort laughed.

"Turducken!" The shriek escaped before I could redirect my thoughts or mouth. "Tom Henn. Wrapped in duct tape. Found inside a turkey." I paused for effect. "Tur…Duck…Hen." My eyes gleamed with morbid pride.

"It ain't duck, darlin." A lanky slack-jawed man pushed into my space. "It doesn't surprise me you'd think that." He continued with a snide attitude. "You're wrong. It's duct - with a *t*." A shower of spittle emphasized the letter.

My hackles went up. I wiped my cheek and reared back for a scathing retort. Lorna grabbed my arm.

"This is my brother, Joey. He's special."

"Damn straight," Joey crowed.

Two officers pulled the turkey away from Tom Henn. Joey was drawn to it like a moth to a flame. Lorna gave me a pleading look. I smiled and waved away my frustration.

"Where did his hickish accent come from?" I asked.

"He downloaded it from a conspiracy theory website."

"The one that sends you a sleeveless t-shirt with membership?"

"Exactly."

The officers tried to fend off the interloper, but Joey would not be deterred. He started monologuing. I caught a few snippets about the history of nylon, how most inflatables are Chinese, and that this one must have surveillance tech woven into the fabric.

"Is that normal?" I asked.

"For Joey it is," Lorna replied. "He lives in our parents' basement."

"I thought he had a job."

"He's worked at the bowling alley since high school." Lorna wrinkled her nose. "Not a go-getter but claims to be an expert in everything. Calls himself a 'blackbelt in verbal jujitsu.'"

"That's a trait of sociopaths."

"Accurate. Challenge him on anything and he yells a bunch of nonsense until you walk away." Lorna rolled her eyes. "He considers that a win."

"Extraverted idiots are the worst."

The laugh is a good distraction, but Joey's behavior is troubling. People like him are exhausting. Some can be dangerous if pushed.

"There's my girl." A husky man with curly black hair emerged from behind a pilgrim and embraced Lorna.

"Hey, Dad." Lorna returned the hug. She wrapped an arm around me. "Dad, this is Alice." She gestured toward her father. "Alice, this is my dad, Benny."

"Wonderful to meet you, Al," Benny said with a broad smile.

"Likewise." I returned the grin.

Benny's smile faded at the sight of the body. "Oh, Margo." He reached for his wife, and she collapsed into his embrace. "Let's go inside and let the police handle things."

* * *

The Harvester home reflected my entire Pinterest list. We climbed the steps to a broad porch that framed a bright red door. Benny led us through the open floor plan, tastefully decorated in earth tones, to a seating area that faced a fieldstone fireplace. I sank into the cushy leather sofa next to Lorna.

"It's the Eve of Gratitude," Benny said. He pointed to Lorna. "What does that mean?"

"Pizza," Lorna exclaimed with a fist pump.

"Not just any pizza," Benny wagged a finger.

"The Harvester Special," Lorna continued in a well-rehearsed schtick. She leaned into me. "Every holiday eve is celebrated with homemade pizza."

"I'm always down for pizza." My stomach growled in agreement.

Benny disappeared into the kitchen, whistling a happy tune. He didn't seem too upset about the dead guy in his holiday display. Margo's a different story. She curled into the overstuffed chair across from us and stared at the floor. Lorna elbowed my arm and handed me a piece of paper.

"What's this?"

"Menu for tomorrow." She pointed to the top. "The Mulberry Grove Thanksgiving Feast."

"The Reenactment?"

"Yeah," Lorna chuckled. "The town pretends it's the first Thanksgiving."

"Candied yams."

"You two talkin' sexy?" Joey leered over my shoulder.

"Jesus!" I jumped in alarm.

"I am God's gift, darlin." He grabbed his crotch. "I got your candy yams right here."

"No, thank you." I wondered how he snuck up like that.

Lorna glossed over her brother's comment and waved the list. "Menu for tomorrow, doofus."

Joey lectured her on the history of yams. Two men come in behind him.

"I found this turkey lurking in the driveway." Sheriff Winkle grinned at a burly man in his fifties.

"Buddy," Margo crossed the room and hugged the newcomer.

"Buddy Todd," Lorna explained. "He owns Memory Lanes, the bowling alley where Joey works. He grew up with my parents and has uncle status."

"Happy Eve of Gratitude, my good man." Benny emerged from the kitchen carrying a beer. "Pizzas are in the oven."

"Grateful for this." Buddy accepted the brew and smiled in our direction. "Good to see you, Lorna."

"You too, Buddy. This is Alice." Lorna gave my shoulder a squeeze.

"Nice to meet you." Buddy tipped the bottle toward me then raised it to his lips.

"Margo, Benny? A quick word before dinner?" Sheriff Winkle asked.

They left the room, and Joey held forth about heat distribution in pizza stones. I tuned out and sifted through magazines on the coffee table. A handsome man smiled up from the Mulberry Grove Gazette. The headline caught my eye.

Henn Ruffles Feathers with Boardwalk Development.

My kind of journalist. Wait, that's turducken guy. I snatched up the paper and skimmed the story.

Tom Henn promised business owners along the Boardwalk, a popular tourist area, he will protect the town's historical integrity and prevent outside interests from reshaping the landscape.

"Henn was good people." Buddy made his way around the sofa and settled into the chair Margo vacated. His eyes were full of sorrow. "Tom promised to keep Mulberry Grove from turning into another tourist trap."

"Is that what got him killed?" I asked.

"Maybe," Buddy sipped his beer. "I can't believe he's gone."

"Ten bucks says he was in that turkey when you dropped me off last night," Joey butted in.

"Time to eat-za da pizza," Benny sang. It brought our conversation to an end.

* * *

"This food baby shall be named Pepperoncini," I announced and patted my overstuffed belly. "That was excellent za."

"Dad prides himself on his intuitive pizza making skills," Lorna said. "But I've caught him searching the internet for recipes."

"I'm surprised your parents are okay with us sharing a room," I shifted topics as we climbed the stairs. "I expected old school."

"You'll see." She stopped in front of a door and reached for the knob.

"Welcome to my adolescence."

Sultry vampires and seductive werewolves glowered from lilac walls. A bookshelf crammed with YA novels separated twin beds clad in zebra print. Lorna tossed her bag on the bed farthest from the door and lifted a stuffed pig from the pillow. "Stinky McBacon and I endured a multitude of rejections in this very room."

"He's a natural therapist. Porcine are known for their inherent compassion."

Lorna collapsed on the bed and snuggled Stinky. I heaved my bag onto the other bed and sat next to her.

"Don't worry." I tickled the pig's chin. "I got your candy yams right here."

* * *

A little mascara, a swipe of lip gloss. I was ready for the new day. Lorna's voice flowed up the stairs. She was heated. I tiptoed to the landing.

"Absolutely not."

"Everyone is counting on you," Benny argued. "Especially this year."

Margo caught me eavesdropping and waved me down. I followed her into the kitchen.

"Happens every year. Sort of a Thanksgiving tradition."

"It's the last time." Lorna caved. "It's disrespectful to Native Americans."

"Understood." Benny pushed a pair of black shoes adorned with brass buckles into Lorna's arms. She stomped out of the room and up the stairs. Moments later, a door slammed.

Margo shook her head. "He knows the whole event is tone deaf for the times." She pulled a variety of fruits and vegetables out of the fridge. "He can't help himself. Could you get that basket, dear?"

I grabbed a wicker basket off the table and placed it next to the pile of food. Margo arranged vegetables around the perimeter and built a mountain of fruit in the middle. She topped it off with a stalk of broccoli.

"Adds interest."

Footsteps clomped down the stairs to announce Lorna's return. Lorna the Pilgrim, that is. Full on English Separatist. I can tell she's miserable. Benny followed in a similar outfit. He hooked the basket with his arm.

"Blessings of the season, daughter."

"Shut up."

"I didn't hear you." Benny cupped his ear.

"Good cheer and glorious bounty," Lorna replied in monotone and accepted the basket.

"Let's rock this feast," Joey blustered in dressed in his version of Native American garb—tight leather pants, moccasins, a beaded necklace, and a single feather attached to the back of his head with a fabric band. He's shirtless. And beyond offensive.

"Good morrow, Squanto," Benny said.

Lorna cringed and offered the basket to her brother. "May our feast create abundance between our people."

Joey rifled through the basket. "It's all wrong." He frowned at the broccoli. "The Indians gave food to the Pilgrims, not the other way around."

"Humor me," Benny clapped his son on the shoulder and scowled at me. "Why isn't Al dressed?"

For the record, I was fully clothed. I inspected my soft cranberry sweater paired with dark jeans and raised an eyebrow at Lorna. She refused to meet my eyes.

"I haven't had a chance to tell her."

"Alice, you're in for a treat." Benny's eyes sparkled with mischief. "You have the honor of representing the Harvester family in Mulberry Grove's Annual Gobbler Waddle."

* * *

"Lookin' good." I assessed my wingspan and tail feathers.

"Mom never lets anyone else wear this." Lorna sighed "But with Tom…"

"Happy to help," I said out of obligation. I smoothed the soft brown fabric that covered my torso with wings in festive hues of red, orange, and yellow. The tail fanned out across my back in the same bold color pattern.

"Don't forget your beak." Lorna held up a latex turkey face attached to a brown hood.

"Yikes," I gasped. "That's realistic."

"Right down to the snood." Lorna grabbed a weird red appendage that hung from the enormous beak.

"Snood?"

Lorna grinned. She enjoyed this way too much. "You're a female bird so yours is small and elegant. Males have elongated snoods."

"Why does that sound suggestive?"

"Because it is. Snoods attract the ladies." Lorna waggled her eyebrows. "They also change colors according to mood."

"Okay, Joey."

Lorna shoved the hood over my head. I adjusted the eye holes, technically nostrils, until I had a clear view.

"The finishing touch." Lorna clasped a string of large fake pearls around my turkey neck.

"Those should attract some good snoodling." I laughed.

"You two ready?" Benny's voice called from downstairs.

"Almost," Lorna shouted. She dropped a pair of turkey feet in front of me. "They go over your shoes."

I wrestled into the talon shaped contraptions. "You expect me to run in these?"

"It'll be fine."

I didn't believe her. It wasn't just the turkey toes. The tights were brutal. Bright yellow spandex with full compression. I did squats and high knees before I waddled to the stairs. The nostrils restricted my vision, so I navigated by feel. The last step was a doozy. My wings flapped desperately as my turkey feet skidded across the wood floor. I slammed beak first into the wall.

"Bravo!" Benny cheered.

Margo applauded and I curtseyed with outstretched wings.

"Ten out of ten." Pilgrim Lorna pulled off my turkey hood and tucked it under my wingpit.

"Let's hit the road." Benny bolted out the door. The heels of his buckle shoes clacked across the porch and down the steps.

We filed out behind him, Margo bringing up the rear of our bizarre parade. The yard looked surreal in the bright, crisp sunshine. Tom's body was gone, but officers still combed the area around deflated pilgrims, flat pumpkins, and one miserable cornucopia.

"I wonder if they know who did it," I whispered to Lorna.

"All aboard the gratitude train." Benny slid open the side door of his minivan.

We clambered into the back seat. Lorna miscalculated the headroom and her hat toppled backwards. I caught it and admired the shiny buckle strapped around the narrow crown.

"Matches your shoes. Didn't women wear bonnets?"

"Yeah, but the First Thanksgiving was mostly men."

"That's not fair."

"The women were dead."

"Speaking of dead…" I eyed her parents. "Are they okay? Your mom's boss was murdered in their front yard just a few hours ago."

Lorna shrugged. A kerfuffle forced Margo to release her claim to the front. She joined us in the cheap seats. Joey calmed down in the passenger seat, and we set off for what I was sure would be an adventure.

* * *

Upon arrival, a grizzled turkey greeted us. His t-shirt advised us to *Just Wing It*. Benny engaged the bird in a serious discussion regarding the event budget.

"Costumes are a source of family pride," Lorna explained as we walked through the crowd of turkeys and farmers milling about the Village Green. "Many were passed down through generations."

"Why are the Farmers creepy?" I jutted my beak at a scarecrow-zombie love child.

"They took a turn several years ago. Less hee-haw, more pitchfork."

"Symbolic pitchforks, I hope."

"The chase is all in good fun, There's pie at the finish."

"What kind?"

"All of them." Lorna considered. "Heavy on the pumpkin, but a good selection from apple to pecan. The full range of creams and meringues too."

"Slice limit?"

"Unlimited for Gobblers."

"I retract all qualms regarding this event."

"Turkeys!" Benny's voice crackled through the loudspeaker. "Report to the starting line. Farmers, you're on deck."

We followed the crowd to a balloon arch over the street at the north corner of the town square.

"This is the start and finish line," Lorna instructed. "Turkeys get a ten second head start. Twice around the square and you'll be done."

"Twice around for pie. Got it."

I warmed up with lunges and jumping jacks before I took my place in the poultry line up.

"Turkeys at the ready," Benny's voice echoed off the buildings. "On your mark...Get set...WADDLE!"

The street flooded with a kaleidoscope of autumnal colors. It was impossible to get anywhere quickly. Wings and beaks pummeled me from every angle. The hood twisted and I was down to one nostril.

"Release the Farmers!" Benny's voice broke through the madness.

Anxiety pushed me forward in long strides to accommodate the wide turkey feet. My right eye was trained through the nostril. I'd be okay if I followed the bird directly in front of me. Two times around, then pie.

Vicious snarls caught me off guard. A rough shove sent me reeling. A turkey toe hooked the curb, and I made a spectacular beak-dive onto the concrete White stars sparked around me. Hot copper filled my mouth. Dazed, I scrambled to my knees. Hands gripped my wings and hauled me roughly across the sidewalk, shredding my tights and what little was left of my dignity. Waves of pain radiated through my body. Would this affect my pie chances?

"You ungrateful bitch." Male voice. Angry.

My blood turned to ice. I strained to see through the nostril. Green suspenders over orange and brown plaid. Pumpkin farmer? I hunkered down to get a look at his face. Good Lord, he was wearing a burlap hood.

"You won't ruin this town." The farmer spit the words through gritted teeth.

He must think I'm Margo. The pieces snapped into place. Margo worked for Tom Henn. This was the murderer. Desperate, I wrestled my arms out of the wings and grasped the inside of the hood. The nostrils realigned and revealed a glint of metal.

"I'm not who you want," I squeaked. "I'm not Margo."

The sounds of laughter and running feet on the street seemed a million miles away. Doesn't anyone see what's happening?

"She'll get the message," the voice growled.

A blur of orange and steel rushed past the nostrils. I curled into a tight ball and braced for the pierce of a sharp blade. Instead, a scuffle erupted in a cacophony of scrapes, grunts, and groans. Something crashed into me. I rolled onto my back, helpless. Rapid footsteps approached. Another blur. A metallic clink. More grunts. A loud *splat* ended the fracas.

"Al!"

A shiny buckle appeared in front of the nostrils. "Lorna?"

"Yeah, it's gonna be fine." Her relieved expression moved into view. "Mom used her aggressive hugging skills."

"She sure packed a wallop." Sheriff Winkle leaned in and gave me a thumbs up.

A tug at the back of my neck released me from the poultry prison. I welcomed the rush of fresh air and took the hood from Lorna. Pumpkin farmer guy is sprawled on the ground in front of me, wrists cuffed behind his back. Margo stood over him, arms folded across her chest.

"Who is that?" my voice shook.

"It's…" Lorna begins.

"Buddy," Joey interrupted. "I knew it the whole time."

"No, you didn't. Mom just told us."

"My brain knew it first."

Benny sidled up to his son. "How about you get a slice or two of pie and save us seats for the Feast?"

Joey loped away. Lorna eyed her father with irritation. She hoisted me up by the wing.

"You okay? Your lip is bleeding."

"Kissed the concrete." I kicked out a yellow human foot. "Turkey toes were sacrificed."

Lorna squeezed my wing. "You need pie."

"Lots of pie."

"You're one lucky turkey." Sheriff Winkle picked up a knife and dropped it into a plastic bag.

Buddy, now unmasked, was escorted to a nearby police car. Lorna, her parents, and I crossed the Village Green toward a display of scrumptious desserts. Turkeys and Farmers, friends once again, stuffed their beaks and faces while they rehashed the Waddle. Nobody seemed to have noticed what happened. That's fine with me. The shock will hit eventually, but right now my goal was to regain human form and eat the entire Thanksgiving menu.

Margo and Benny flanked Joey at the picnic table. Lorna placed her hat in the seat across from her mother. I plunked the turkey head next to it.

"Al wants to change clothes."

"The Reenactment starts in five minutes." Benny tossed his keys across the table.

* * *

Minivans are not meant to be dressing rooms. Crouched on the floor, I wiggled out of the costume. My sore muscles protested, but I emerged a happier woman. Lorna was distraught.

"I have to stay a pilgrim." She patted my soft sweater.

"Good cheer, my lady. Tis thee who must bestow the broccoli of peace upon the masses."

"Huzzah," Lorna responded weakly. "Your lip is bleeding again."

We returned to the joyful atmosphere of the Village Green. My mouth watered at the variety of Thanksgiving delicacies set up next to the desserts. Benny bustled over with Lorna's hat.

"It's time for the blessing. The native is restless."

Joey bounced up and down near the buffet, the basket of food dangled from his arm. Lorna shoved the hat onto her head and frowned.

"This won't take long," she promised and trailed after her father.

A quick scan of the tables located the turkey head. Margo was in the middle of an animated conversation with her friends. She smiled at my approach.

"How are you, dear? I've been filling everyone in."

"I'm fine, happy to be human again."

Polite chuckles allowed me to get settled before the inevitable interrogation began. Margo sensed my discomfort and made a preemptive move.

"The Feast is about to start." She pointed to her family lined up by the buffet.

Right on cue, Benny greeted the crowd. "Good cheer, one and all. Welcome to Mulberry Grove's Annual Thanksgiving Feast."

Squanto Joey and Pilgrim Lorna stepped forward. They turned to face each other.

"May the blessings of this feast foretell a prosperous year to come." Benny spread his arms, as if embracing the entire town.

Squanto held the basket in outstretched hands. The Pilgrim accepted the generous offer. The townsfolk cheered the completed transaction. Benny reached his palms to the sky in a show of gratitude while Joey performed a series of high kicks. Lorna watched in bemusement.

"Let the Feast begin," Benny shouted.

The table next to the buffet was already empty, its inhabitants busy piling their plates. It would be a while before the line went down. The pilgrims returned to the table and Lorna grasped my hand. Margo took the opportunity to continue the Buddy report.

"It came together for me right before the race." Margo leaned toward her friends. "Last night, the sheriff told us it was Joey's handwriting on the pie box found with Tom."

"Joey admitted it," Benny added. "He wrote *Ungrateful Bastard* because someone ate the last slice."

"But he didn't murder Tom," Margo said.

"There's no way," Benny agreed. "He worked all evening. Buddy dropped him off around midnight. He didn't leave the house after that."

Margo nodded. "When we arrived today, I helped unbox pies. I recalled that Joey blamed Buddy for eating his pie. He wrote the insult on the box and put it in Buddy's office. That was the night Tom was killed." Her brown eyes shone with tears.

"Buddy locks his office every night, so he was the only one with access to the box," Benny said.

"I told the Sheriff, but the race had already started." Margo reached for my free hand. "We didn't know Buddy was one of the farmers until Lorna saw you on the ground."

"Why would Buddy want to hurt you, Margo?"

"Money. Tom worked tirelessly to preserve this town. He was fighting a big developer who wants to turn the Boardwalk into a bunch of tacky souvenir shops. Buddy claimed to support the community, but Tom believed he was negotiating with the developer, too. Memory Lanes is a Boardwalk hot spot. Tom confronted Buddy a few days ago."

"Buddy assumed you would continue Tom's fight."

"He assumed right. I will."

Joey appeared behind his parents with a heaping plate of food. He pushed Benny into the adjacent seat and squeezed into the chair between them.

"So much for waiting your turn." Lorna eyed his full plate.

"Get it before it's gone." Joey replied through a mouthful of stuffing.

"Excellent thinking, son."

"Oh, my God, Dad," Lorna was not happy.

"What?"

"Why do you enable his stupidity?"

Benny tilted his head. "We support both of our children." He waved toward me.

I was stunned. Lorna ignited in silent fury. Margo acted like she missed the exchange. Joey gnashed down on a turkey leg. Benny pulled his wife to her feet, and they headed for the buffet.

"Happens every visit," Lorna said. "I'd hoped to get through this one unscathed."

"Let's recap the last twenty-four hours." I dabbed my split lip. "We discovered a turducken murder, had a pizza party with the murderer, were forced into costume, I got attacked while wearing said costume, by said murderer." I raised my eyebrows for effect. "And, I have yet to receive a single slice of pie for my troubles."

"Duly noted." Lorna laughed and wrapped her arm around me.

"We were scathed from the beginning." I rested my head on Lorna's shoulder. "But you know what? It's been the best Thanksgiving of my life." I smiled at her. "Now, let's eat pie."

Quick Black Beans

Combine the following ingredients in either a large bowl to be served at room temperature or chilled, or in a pot to be heated:

(2) 15.5 ounce cans of black beans, mostly drained

1 tsp ground cumin

½ tsp chili powder

½ tsp granulated garlic

¼ tsp onion powder

¼ tsp paprika

*1/2 tsp salt if using no salt added beans, otherwise use less to your taste

grinds of black pepper or dashes of cayenne powder

Serve with tortilla chips and salsa as an appetizer, or 5 individual half cup portions.

Easy as Pie

Mike Rusetsky

"Jeez, now what?" Bruiser asked, watching his younger brother drag a burlap sack across the threshold. The thing must've been heavy, the way Davey strained under its weight.

"It's potatoes, Big B! A whole doggone sack of 'em!"

Bruiser sighed and slammed the register shut. Once again, he had to play the responsible big brother to Davey's overexcited younger self. Thank goodness no customers were around to witness this, or their goose would've been cooked.

"Davey, how many times I told ya? Don't be carrying stolen goods through the front door! Customers could've seen you. Jeez, do you want me to get fired my first week on the job?"

Davey's face dropped, and he looked away in shame. "I'm sorry, Bruiser. Just got excited, is all."

"Alright, well… Don't be a weeping willow about it. Let me help you with that."

Bruiser tried to lift the sack off the floor and found it shockingly heavy. "Well, hot dog," he muttered, and put his back into it.

"I told ya, didn't I? Them taters is heavy as heck!"

"*Are* heavy. Don't mangle words, little brother. I promised Ma to learn ya proper!"

"Sorry, Big B. Thanks for helping out!"

"Yeah, yeah…"

Bruiser hoisted the sack onto his shoulders and shakily crossed the length of the cigarette store. The floorboards creaked a complaint with every step. "Get the back door for me, would ya?"

Davey obliged and Bruiser slipped through, laboring under the load. Having hidden it in the supply room out back, where he and Davey spent the last few nights, he returned to the store.

"I'm not saying you did bad, baby brother. We'll be eating good for a month at least. But dang!" He wiped the sweat off his brow. "Next time, maybe steal us a carton of milk instead."

Davey looked pouty again. "I didn't see no milk though, Bruiser. Only that there tater sack. Fell off the back of a farmer's truck. I was the first one to it."

His brother gave him a comforting pat on the shoulder. "There, there. You were thinking of family and did your best. Look, we just broke out of Franklin, what—five days ago? We can't be busted doing petty theft in the light of day. I ain't going back there again. Unless maybe *you* want to?"

The question hung heavy, like a sack of potatoes, between them. Davey shook his head emphatically, and Bruiser nodded. "That's what I thought. Bet Warden Jackson would *love* to have us back. Maybe some of our fellow inmates would, too. I say, we've started a whole new life now! I got me a proper job, in this here cigarette shop. That's stability, Davey. Folks will always need their tobacco, see. Long term plans are what we need, and the kind of risk you took today, that'll land us back in Franklin."

"I know," Davey sighed. His face looked mournful. Bruiser had to ignore his own aching heart at the sight of it. He'd promised their mother to take care of Davey, years ago. Dusty "Big" Bruiser always lived up to his promises.

The front doorbell dinged, signaling a customer. Bruiser waved Davey off and cleared his throat before calling out to the stranger.

"Morning, sir!"

"Hey there, fella. I'll take today's paper and a pack of Lucky's."

Bruiser nodded acknowledgment and reached for the shelf of Lucky Strikes behind him. Handing the stranger his smokes, Bruiser paused, examined him for the first time. He noted the man's rolled up white sleeves, the driving gloves, and the old-fashioned rounded newsboy cap… he decided to chance it.

"Say, stranger. Ain't I seen you in here yesterday? And the day before, maybe?"

The visitor squinted his eyes at Bruiser. "Yeah, and what of it? Can't a man buy his news of the day and smokes in peace?"

Bruiser broke into a reassuring grin. "That he can, mister! I'm just noticing, though, you seem to live around here. My brother and I just moved to the neighborhood."

The man handed his two dollars to Bruiser, picked up his newspaper and cigarettes. "I work around here, that's for sure. Been driving the same delivery route for years."

"No kiddin'? Who you drive for, if it ain't too nosy a question?"

The stranger measured Bruiser with his eyes, then must have decided the lad was alright. "Madam Chalkby's Baking Shoppe." He lit a cigarette off his match. He sucked in the smoke, then released a puffy cloud. Leaning on the counter, he rested a long brass key atop it.

Bruiser coughed at the smoke, but still noticed the man's key, which must've been for his delivery vehicle. He figured a friendly chat could be useful; couldn't hurt to know the clientele better. You never knew what the locals could help you with, and vice versa. He didn't quite know what "vice versa" meant, but his Ma used to say it sometimes, and she never steered him wrong.

"Well, I'll be! You deliver all those tasty baked goods, do ya?" Bruiser smiled. "What's the hot ticket item now? So close to Thanksgiving."

"*Too* close if you ask me, pal. I might be doing overtime, not that Madam Chalkby will pay me for it."

"Tough luck, friend."

"Yeah, I'll live." Another smoke cloud bloomed. "Between you and me: she's got me delivering this giant order tomorrow, not just here but all over the county! I might have to refuel on petrol, that's how much ground I gotta cover."

He shook his head in disgust, and Bruiser did his best to empathize, and to disguise his growing interest. "Shucks, mister. That's a shame."

"Well, that's life for ya. Some days these Lucky Strikes are the only thing worth looking forward to anymore."

"You must make a lot of folks happy, though! All those sweet treats headin' their way?"

The man made a face like he just sucked a lemon. "Lots of rich folks' homes. Their butlers and servants pick up the orders, then set them out at supper time. Yep, rich folks and their fancy guests, is who eats Madam Chalkby's goodies. Or can afford to, anyway."

Bruiser nodded, his mind turning over quickly. He'd been forming a plan in his head and needed only a few more pieces to build something cohesive from the jumbled pile.

"Say, what kind of order you got tomorrow? Maybe I can lend a hand. My little brother's a jobless lazy head, he might help you hit some of the local spots."

But the man shook his head and frowned again. "I wish I could, pal but all those orders, they gotta be delivered by official personnel. The truck's got 'Madam Chalkby's Baking Shoppe' painted on the side. That's who's gotta drive and drop off all them pies tomorrow."

At the mention of pies, something happened inside Bruiser's mouth. It felt very wet, very quickly. He swallowed, but the feeling didn't go away. "Pie?" he said cautiously. "What kind of pie?"

"All kinds," the man said. He was almost done with his cigarette and was now consulting his pocket watch. Bruiser didn't have long with him, and he knew it. "Pumpkin Pie. Cherry Pie. Apple, too. But her Thanksgiving specialty, this and every year, is Kentucky Pecan Pie."

Bruiser almost had to pinch himself not to whimper. "Pecan, did you say?" he asked, breathless for he could barely speak. The sense memory and flavor of his Ma's signature dish—warm, chewy pecan pie had overtaken him. It was all he could do not to drool in front of this man. Which would not be good customer service.

"Gooey-est pie I ever tasted!" the driver said, stubbing out his cigarette. "Well, the load won't go deliver itself. I best be about it."

The man grabbed the ignition key off the counter and slipped it back in his pocket.

"Just one last question, sir. If'n ya don't mind."

Slightly annoyed, but mollified now that he got his first cigarette of the day, the stranger looked back from his newsboy cap. "Shoot, son, but then I gotta make like a river and run."

Bruiser grinned, feeling as if that was the polite reaction to the man's quip. "You won't by chance be delivering any of those pies to Franklin House, will ya?"

The stranger stared for a moment, then broke out in raucous laughter. "God no, lad! That's poor folk country. Franklin House, on Tenth Street and Pauper's Way?" When Bruiser nodded, the man chuckled. "No way, brother. Them boys will just have to go hungry for Thanksgiving. Or eat whatever slop they're fed. No, Madam Chalkby's Baking Shoppe is for refined, upstanding members of society. Not the gutter snipes in Franklin."

Bruiser's hand curled into a fist under the counter, but he kept his breathing measured. "Way of the world, eh, mister?"

The customer nodded and tapped the rolled-up newspaper twice on the counter. "Sure is, young man. You take care now!"

"You do likewise," Bruiser nodded, approximating a friendly face. Inside him, a storm was brewing. As soon as the visitor left, he shouted Davey's name so loud the glass display case nearly sprung a crack.

* * *

"Wait, so what's the plan?" Davey scratched the back of his neck.

"It's a heist, little brother. We're doing an honest-to-goodness criminal caper!"

Davey frowned. "But… didn't you just tell me to stay off the streets during the day?"

"Never mind all that. Now I got justice pumpin' in my veins! We gotta do something, especially now we got the means to do it."

"I don't get it, Big B. How come you was mad at me for some taters, but now you want to steal a whole *truck*?"

"*Inside* voice, Davey!" Bruiser hissed and lowered his own. "Now look here. This man I just met, he's a delivery driver. I noted the time he came in, eight o'clock on the dot. Man wanted his morning paper and his Lucky's."

"What's *that*?"

"Delicious cigarettes all the doctors are recommending. That's not important right now! You know what's even more delicious than morning smokes?"

"Pie?" Davey guessed, this being the third time they've discussed it.

"Pie!" Bruiser smiled. "Pumpkin Pie. Cherry Pie. Apple Pie. Of particular interest to us: Kentucky Pecan Pie."

Davey's cheeks parted in a dreamy smile. "Ooh... that sounds real good."

"Don't it, though? Just like Ma used to make! Doubt if you remember, being a squirt when she passed... think of it, Davey. We can taste it again! We already know when the pies will be in our vicinity."

"How do we know that? You ain't a fortune teller."

Bruiser rolled his eyes. "Come on, baby brother! Put your thinkin' cap on! I just told ya: the delivery man has a daily routine. Stuff he does every day, like one of Ford's conveyor machines. Guess who's part of that routine?"

"Pie?"

"No, Davey! Not pie! I mean—yes, pie but *us*, baby brother! We're his first stop, before he even sets out to deliver a single order. With tomorrow being Thanksgiving, he's got a mighty huge order to shell out. Bet your bottom dollar he'll be stoppin' off here for his first Lucky Strike. That's when *we* strike!"

Davey looked unconvinced, so Bruiser tried again. "The driver comes in to buy his newspaper and cigarettes. I won't be behind the counter as usual."

"You won't?"

"Nope, because someone will sneak his engine key off the counter and bring it over to where I'll be waiting. Outside, by his truck."

"Swell! Then we eat pie?"

"Not yet! We get in that truck and abscond with the whole load."

"Abs-cone?"

"It means *steal*, Davey. We're gonna steal all the pies, and the truck."

"What we need the truck for?"

"Cause that's the most efficient way to move the *pies*, seein' as how they're already stored there. Don't interrupt me, Davey."

"Sorry."

Bruiser winced, then continued. "By the time the driver realizes there's nobody home at the smoke shop, we'll be long gone. We'll have all the Kentucky Pecan Pie we could ever want!"

He still didn't think Davey understood, judging by his brother's screwed up lips and knotted eyebrows. "Where are we gonna go, Big B? Is that your new job, to deliver pies?"

This time, he wasn't too far off. Bruiser's face relaxed into a soft smile. "Sorta. We'll stop by just one location on our way out of town. I was thinking we might drop by Franklin House."

As expected, Davey's eyes grew wide. "Bruiser! I thought we wouldn't ever go back there! You said…"

"I know what I said but also, talking to this driver man… well, it didn't seem right that all these gussied up folk was gonna munch on pie this Thanksgiving, and our old pals at Franklin would just be starin' out their windows, hungry as ever."

"Maybe Warden Jackson will give them something…"

Bruiser snapped at him. "Do you remember Warden Jackson giving a hoot about us before? Orderin' sweets on any holiday at all?"

"We got them caramel apples last Christmas…"

Bruiser sighed. "That's right… okay, well—before that, though? That's not a happy place with tasty memories, Davey. The least we can do before bidding this Godforsaken town good-bye, is to drop off some pie to our fellow suffering brothers."

"And then we go?"

"And then we go. Easy as… you know. Just you and me, driving into the sunset. Well… it'll be about eight-thirty in the morning, but you know what I mean. We're leaving this place behind."

Davey nodded, seeming to come to a decision. "Think I got it now, Big B."

"You do?"

"Yeah. One thing's still confusin' me."

"Shoot, partner."

"How are we gonna get the key to that man's truck?"

A smile oozed its way onto Bruiser's face. "That's where *you* come in, baby brother."

* * *

The next morning dawned, and the plan was set in motion. Bruiser had packed both of their rucksacks full of provisions and what few belongings they had, and by 7:50 he was crouched in the alley next to the smoke shop. He'd secreted Davey away inside the store in what he termed his "special hiding place." He only hoped Davey's youthful eagerness wouldn't give up the jig for both of them.

To his massive relief, at 7:58 Bruiser heard a large piston engine growl down the street. He poked out his head to see the big cloth-covered truck pulling up next to the store. His heart raced as he watched the delivery driver, clad in the same newsboy cap but with a fresh brown shirt on, kill the engine and hop out, then head inside the shop. Bruiser whispered a nervous "Our Father," which did not register as ironic to him, left the alley, and casually approached the unmanned truck.

Inside, the driver glanced around an apparently empty store.

"Say there, fella! You in here? Got a customer!"

He announced himself once more before his eye caught a piece of paper lying on top of the counter. Moving closer, he saw a message had been scrawled with someone's unpracticed hand.

> *Deer Sir,*
> *I have steppd out fer the time beeing. Pleez help yerself to*
> *yor uzuall order. Leeve the $2 on kounter and I will see you*

twomorrow. Happey Thankz-Giving!
Sinceriously,
Dusty Bruiser

As the man puzzled over the letter, which was seemingly addressed to him, he did not pay heed enough to notice a burlap sack standing a foot away, propped against the counter. The man had to read the message again, mouthing along with the awkward verbiage, and it was during his second attempt that a human hand slowly emerged from the top of the sack.

"Well shoot, I guess that fella really trusts me. I like that," he said aloud, which prompted the hand to whip back inside the burlap. The driver whistled a tune as he paced around the shop and looked at the shelves with refreshed interest. "Ah, better not get him in trouble, I suppose," he said, reconsidered something, then tossed his truck's engine key onto the countertop, next to his stack of eight quarters. When he circled around the counter and neared the back wall, where the Lucky Strike shelf awaited him, he heard a distinct rustling sound come from behind.

Turning back, he saw the door remained closed and nobody else had entered the shop. "Silly ole me. Better get my puffs and get going." He reached for his Lucky's and shook out the first cigarette of the morning. It would be a long day, and he might as well…

The bell atop the front door clanged, making the man jump.

Nobody there. Again.

"Just what in Sam Hill…"

As he rounded the counter and stood in the middle of the shop, he found himself to be the only person present. Except now, the potato sack that had been stored upright was lying at his feet, crumpled up and bereft of any root vegetables.

"That corn liquor got me good last night, didn't it?" he murmured to himself. No matter, he had a job to do and a long day ahead of him. Reaching for his key on the counter, he grasped nothing but the misspelled note and his two dollars in change. As he searched the keyless countertop, he heard the roar of an engine outside.

"You little rascal!" he cried and scurried towards the exit.

* * *

The engine coughed at Bruiser, and he didn't think it would turn over. Or maybe he was doing it wrong? He'd only driven a car once, when his father had been alive, and Ma had given him such what-for poor Dad didn't dare do it again. Not that it mattered anymore, with both long gone…

Another hacking cough, and the engine rumbled awake.

"Thank goodness!" Davey said. Bruiser gave his brother a reassuring elbow nudge, then watched Davey's face grow terrified.

"The man! He's running, Big B!"

Sure enough, the driver appeared in the doorway of the smoke shop, the half-burnt cigarette hanging from a mouth that was shaping some mighty foul language in their address.

"Sorry, can't hear ya! Engine's too loud!" Bruiser yelled, then kicked the truck into first gear. Or what he was pretty *sure* was the first gear. Jeez, he thought, don't let me forget which way them gears are arranged.

The truck jerked forward, the man giving chase and shouting profanities. Bruiser switched into second, and the gears allowed it, with only a mild cranky groan. Davey whooped next to him as they gained speed, and by the time Bruiser slid the stick into third gear, they were cruising down the street at a blistering twenty-five miles an hour. At least! It was exhilarating: the aroma of the pies mixing with the animal smells on the sidewalk and the breeze throwing his hair amess.

"Yee-haw!" Bruiser shouted into the rushing wind and sunshine. "Good-bye, old stinky town!" He hugged his brother with one arm. "Or should I say: good-*pie*!"

They howled with easy laughter, their future bright as the day all around them.

He had to swerve to avoid a hapless fruit vendor whose cart was angled off the sidewalk and into Bruiser's driving lane.

"Be careful! This thing's fast," said Davey.

His heart hammered from the near miss. Bruiser nodded. "Let's make a quick stop by Franklin House and then let's blow this popsicle stand."

Davey gave a questioning look. "Popsicle stand… I thought we was stealin' pie?"

* * *

There was no time to waste. Their rucksacks were stuffed to the brim with emergency potatoes, and soon their bellies would be stuffed with pie. Bruiser saw the future, and it was bright… though not quite clear. Doubts plagued him—since they were wanted men now, twice over, how far must they travel to outrun the law? Carjacking was a serious crime, not to mention the elicit cargo violation… or pie-olation. He grinned to himself, feeling giddy.

Let them look for him and Davey! They can try. Even if caught, and if they have the gall to charge him with each pie as a separate crime… this would all be worth it. Because life inside Franklin was no life at all for either of them. Now at least they had each other, the open air and all the pie they could ever stuff down their pie-holes. Bruiser felt lighter than a henfeather as he took the left turn onto Pauper's Way. The gates of Franklin House loomed a block away, and he braced his body for impact.

"Hold on and sit still, Davey! I'm gonna ram that gate."

"Okay, I trust you!"

As that statement echoed in Bruiser's mind, the tall wooden gates bearing the initials "F.H." rushed at them. He briefly wondered what would happen if the gates were reinforced with wrought iron on the inside. He'd never had the occasion to check them out before. Oh well, too late to worry about that now.

Weathered lumber exploded as they tore through the gates, rocking the truck on impact, but they made it through. Next order of business was to hit the brakes immediately, unless Bruiser wanted to rip a hole in Franklin House itself. He spun the wheel, fishtailing the truck, regretfully heard some of the pies slide around and fall in the back. Acceptable losses, Bruiser thought, but he hoped those were rhubarb, and not his beloved pecan.

Finally, the truck slid to a stop, mere inches away from the brick-laid wall of Franklin's west wing. Bruiser exhaled with relief. Davey shouted "Wee!" next to him, maybe a little too full of glee.

"Okay, let's start offloading pies. We'll give 'em some of each, so they can get an assortment."

"You said a bad word!"

"No, I said 'assortment.'"

"I'd tell Ma if she was still around."

Bruiser didn't have time for this. He moved to the back of the truck. "Come on, Davey! The pies!"

By the time they jumped off the rear of the truck bed, both their arms stacked with multiple flavored pies, they encountered a severe-looking woman glaring at them from inside a nun's habit.

"Oh, crud. It's Warden Jackson!" Davey whispered, and Bruiser's heart sank at those words.

"Goodness! My… goodness gracious!" the woman kept saying, seemingly frozen in the building's doorway where she stood.

"Good morning, House Mother Jackson!" Bruiser looked at her through the stacks of pies. He vaguely considered dropping them and hauling tail down the street, but there was Davey to think about. Besides, something in the woman's face gave him reason for pause.

"Goodness… It's you! My precious Bruiser boys!"

She clasped at her chest, and for one scary second Bruiser thought he'd given her a heart attack. It was merely a gesture, and she fluttered towards them, gathered both brothers into her arms, despite the pies in the way.

"I didn't think I'd ever see you again!" she cooed. Bruiser felt strange at these words. He was never missed by anyone before.

"Big B got a job in town!" Davey said.

"Did he, now?" She sounded impressed, yet her eyes were full of glistening tears. Nobody but their Ma had ever shed tears on their behalf. Had he misread this whole place, and the authorities who ran it?

"I wanted to stop by," Bruiser offered. He felt oddly numb. "Share some pie with the other boys. I know you all can't afford to give us sweets, so I figured…"

She gently shushed him and drew them closer to herself. "You are mere children," she whispered. "It's *us* who have the duty of care for *you*."

"I'm almost fifteen now, House Mother."

"Your brother is barely ten. Is this the kind of life you want to give him? Running vehicles into buildings?"

Bruiser heaved a sigh. It was not the kind of life he wanted, for himself or for Davey.

"*There*, officer! There's the criminal!"

Their three-fold embrace dissolved at the sound of the voice, which Bruiser knew all too well. The delivery driver stood in what used to be the main gates, accompanied by another man, who was dressed as a uniformed officer of the law. Because that's who he was, Bruiser realized.

"Uh-oh," Davey said next to him.

"It's true," Bruiser spoke up. "We're the culprits. I neglected my job duties at the shop and stole this gentleman's truck. Then we delivered some sweets to our friends here at the Franklin House orphanage."

The officer and the delivery driver walked towards them as he spoke, but with less conviction now. They looked from the rumbling truck to the defiant nun to the two kids, less certain on how to proceed.

"You can arrest me if you wish, sir. I'm a wanted man already, and this here heist… it sure adds to my criminal record."

"You're a kid," the officer said. At these words, the delivery driver removed his newsboy cap in consternation. "The only thing you're guilty of is running away from your orphanage and breaking curfew."

"But…" Bruiser began, yet the officer shook his head.

"House Mother Jackson reported you two missing the night you… ran off. She was worried sick about you boys."

Again, that odd feeling inside Bruiser. She was really worried? About them?

"How about we all discuss this inside, fellas?" the nun proposed. "I'm afraid I can't offer you a drink. But…" she glanced at Bruiser and smiled. "I reckon we can rustle up some pie."

Gelatin and Soda
Stephen M. Pierce

The man walked through the rehabilitation center, holding his Thanksgiving meal in the palm of his hand. There would be no feasting this year. His wife and daughter were hundreds of miles away, enjoying a warm afternoon with his in-laws, but someone had to be with his mother.

He looked straight ahead as screams surrounded him. Some of the guests were barely lucid, while others retained enough wits to be angry at everyone. The nurses only stopped in their rounds long enough to give him a pitying stare, like he was a child lost in a warzone. He smiled blandly and clutched the clear cake carrier to his chest.

The door had a plastic tag reading "Sandra King." An imperious voice came from within.

"I can't find my shoe, Julian."

He spent hours driving here, and before even a greeting left his mother's lips, he was given a problem to solve.

"Happy Thanksgiving to you, too."

He stepped forward and confronted Sandra in her bed. When he was a child, older cousins showed him *The Thing*, and he had nightmares for weeks where he fused with the bed where he slept, skin and mattress becoming a uniform mass. He hated how readily that thought jumped to mind now.

She'd come here for the first time a month ago after a bad fall. Since then, he and Sandra had gone through the carousel of hospital to rehab center, back home and then to the hospital again as symptoms resurfaced. She was always overconfident about her health. Julian was elected to be on call because he worked from home. It was unsustainable, but that conversation was difficult to have when Sandra was more concerned about minor issues.

"I need my shoe," Sandra said. "I have physical therapy in three hours."

"We'll find it," Julian pulled a chair beside her bed. "Can we eat first?"

He placed the cake carrier on the small table that reached across her like a robot giving an embrace, then lifted the plastic dome. Inside was a brown ring of gelatin with flecks of pineapple and pecan suspended inside.

"My favorite," Sandra's wrinkled face broke out in a rare smile. "Did you make this yourself?"

"Even better," he placed disposable spoons and plates on the table. "Your granddaughter made it, with my instructions."

"That's lovely. Make sure she knows she's brightened my day."

Julian's daughter loved Sandra, perhaps more than he did, but it was easy to forget how differently they remembered her. Julian still had mental images of Sandra driving into town, taking the girl out for ice cream, looking like she could fell a tree with her pinky finger, but all his daughter's remaining memories were of her in a chair, trapped in a dirty home. Yet when Sandra asked Lily if she remembered those days in the sun, she always said yes.

He raised his spoon, intending to scoop out a portion of the gelatin, when Sandra grabbed his hand.

"I mean it about the shoe," she said. "It's got me so torn up I don't think I can stomach a bite until it's found."

"You're serious."

"I called you non stop this morning," she said. "If you picked up, you'd know."

"I was driving! What did you want me to do? Crash into a minivan going eighty miles an hour?"

"No, but if you'd listened to my messages, you would have known to drop by the house and make sure it hadn't been left over there."

"I didn't even think about the house," he shook his head. "It's Thanksgiving. I just wanted to see you."

The truth was he wasn't prepared to check in on the rat colony in his mother's old garden shed. On his last visit, they'd managed to develop a primitive Feudalist system.

"Anyway, it couldn't be at the house," he continued. "You were wearing both your shoes when I brought you here."

"Well, I thought they were here last night, but now there's just the one!"

He glanced at the foot of the bed, where one floral-patterned shoe sat solitary and stoic. Perhaps its partner was in another state now, feasting on turkey and popovers.

"Well, where have you looked for it?"

"I glanced around the room a little," Sandra frowned. "I need you to run a full search."

He stood and choked down a groan. "I'll get a nurse."

The woman who entered had shaved hair and hoop earrings, but these were the only personal touches to her uniform. Before Julian could even explain the situation, she clutched a hand to her chest.

"What on earth is that?"

Julian followed her gaze to his Thanksgiving dish, which seemed to vibrate with menace.

"It's a Coca-Cola salad," he said. "Well, one of my wife's coworkers is boycotting Coke, so I guess you'd call it a Pepsi salad. Should taste similar enough though."

"Sure, but…" the nurse trailed off, as if she realized we were speaking two languages. "Why?"

"Her jaws are pretty weak now, so—"

"No, I mean," she gestured forcefully at the desert. "*Why?*"

"I don't know, it's just something my grandmother used to make," he turned to Sandra. "Where'd she get the recipe?"

"Some cookbook. I tried to track it down years ago, but I think we gave it away during the move," she scratched her head. "Why don't you try some, Monique?"

"No, thanks, I'm trying to cut back on sugar," she looked away and winced, "Anyway, what's this about a missing shoe?"

Sandra explained the issue, but Monique didn't seem convinced. She took Julian aside. "Are you sure she didn't forget where it was?"

"She's shown no signs of dementia or Alzheimer's," I said. "Maybe this could be the onset, but for now I believe her. Let's search the room and get her off my back, okay?"

She nodded and we tore through the room. Julian dug through Sandra's blankets while Monique peered behind the furniture and checked the industrial-size bathroom. She even looked in the trash can. It was nowhere to be found.

"I just don't get it," Julian said. "If they'd taken both shoes, I'd sort of understand. But one?"

Monique shrugged. "I can at least tell you we don't have any peglegged pirates around here."

"Even then," he smiled. "I don't think they'd want footwear covered in pansies."

"It must be some unfortunate accident," Sandra waved her hand. "Maybe one of the janitors accidentally picked it up in a pile of sheets and took it to the laundry. Why don't you run down there and ask, Julian?"

When Sandra said, "why don't you", she typically meant, "you'd better get up and do this, or you'll hear about it for the rest of your life." Julian knew it would be quicker to follow along than to argue.

"Can you point me there, Monique?" he asked.

"Sure, it's just down the hall."

They started for the door, but Sandra cleared her throat, showing impressive respiration for a woman with breathing problems.

"You're not planning to leave that behind? The smell will drive me crazy."

Julian glanced at Monique, but she was too busy stifling her laughter to be sympathetic. He turned and grabbed the Pepsi salad, covering it with the dome again, and followed Monique into the hall. The nurse shut the door behind them and frowned.

"Listen, she's your mom. I know you've gotta do whatever you have to. Sometimes she can be a little harsh with the staff. I wouldn't be shocked if someone grabbed that shoe and chucked it in a gutter."

She turned to lead the way, but Julian stood in the hallway for a moment, holding the Pepsi salad and listening to the tail end of an old man's non-exhaustive list of all the people who wronged him that day. He wondered how many people in this building stopped to be grateful for anything. He imagined the overworked and underpaid nurses lacked the time to do it.

He trailed after Monique, reflecting on her words. His mother could have rubbed someone the wrong way, but he was still hung up on the remaining shoe. If someone's goal was to get back at Sandra, why not take both? They had been placed together. It would have taken no extra effort.

He hadn't figured it out by the time Monique shoved him into the laundry room and disappeared. A blonde, middle-aged woman was packing white sheets into an exhausted machine, but she stopped and raised her eyebrow.

"Excuse me," Julian set the dessert on a nearby dryer. "Have you found a shoe in the laundry? Floral-patterned?"

"Last night's stuff is still in that cart." She had a harsh, smoker's voice. "Have at it."

Julian muttered curses under his breath as he dug through the cart, essentially a basket on wheels. He'd seen plenty of cop shows where murderers sneaked out bodies using carts like this, but the strangest thing he found inside was a jockstrap. He stepped away from the cart, trying to forget he'd touched it. No shoe.

The washing machine powered on and began to shake with surprising violence. The woman rubbed her hands together and glanced at the dessert in the cake carrier.

"Is that a Coca-Cola salad?"

"Thank you," Julian said. "Everyone else today has looked at it like it was a bomb. It was made with Pepsi though, not Coke."

She wrinkled her nose. "I hate Pepsi. Might as well drink motor oil. Get that thing out of my sight."

Julian couldn't leave the room fast enough. He'd only been gone a few minutes, but the hallway was now alive with activity. An ambulance was parked out front. EMTs entered a room, but everyone carried on as if it were only a mail truck visiting. Through a large row of windows, he locked eyes with a man in the physical therapy room, who clutched his walker as a woman guided him down a taped line that ran parallel to the hallway.

A striking man in a suit stepped out of his office and approached Julian, his eyebrow raised at the sight of his dessert.

"You haven't touched that thing since I saw you in the lobby," he said. "Do you need help?"

"No, my mom just won't eat it until I find her missing shoe."

"Ah, you're Sandra King's son," a strange smile played on his face. "Come in my office. We'll talk about it."

Julian wasn't sure what this man could do for him, but he was willing to try anything. It was only after he entered the office he realized he was speaking to the rehab facility's director, Bill Dawes.

Bill returned with a few sheets of paper he'd printed off, then grabbed a teapot from a side table. He poured himself a cup, his pulled back hair making his face taut and concentrated.

"So, what's all this about a stolen shoe?"

"I don't know it's stolen," Julian muttered. "It could have gotten lost. I'm just trying to find—"

"I know the things people say," Bill put back the teapot, not offering Julian any. "Anytime a shirt or sock disappears, there must be a cabal of black-market clothing traders operating out of my clinic. Well believe me, that's nonsense."

"Honestly, I didn't think—"

"And even if it were true!" Bill pointed a finger at the heavens. "We wouldn't steal one shoe. Who's going to buy that? It would have been the pair or nothing at all."

"With all respect, Mr. Dawes," Julian said. "I feel like your protests are a little specific."

Bill watched Julian and sipped his tea. The room behind him was meticulously put together, with file cabinets, framed diplomas, and family photos arranged equidistant from each other. It only made Julian more curious about what was hidden inside.

He nodded at the cake carrier. "I've been meaning to ask. What's that thing?"

"This?" Julian raised the lid. "It's a Pepsi salad."

"Is it edible?"

"Give me a break," he slammed down the lid. "I'm sure you have a weird family meal for Thanksgiving."

"I don't celebrate," Bill said. "I'm Cherokee. The holiday means something very different to people like me."

A brief silence passed as Bill sipped his tea. Julian felt he'd stepped on a land mine.

"Well, I think the broad idea of Thanksgiving can be appreciated by everybody," he said, staring out the far window. "It's important to remember what you have to be thankful for."

"You know, I was just telling that to the nurses," Bill smiled. "When you spend all your time complaining about what you don't have, you lose track of what you've got. Just look at me. I've got a lovely family, a well-paying job, and I'm thankful for every patient here. When I remember that, life feels so much kinder."

"I imagine you've got to have those things before you can be thankful for them."

"Don't you start," Bill shook his head. "What about you? I know you can think of something."

Julian opened his mouth to speak, but his throat was empty. He was miles away from his wife and daughter, in a depressing building, going on a wild goose chase when he should have been enjoying a meal. His family heritage was apparently a laughingstock, and he would likely be reminded of this day as one of a successive train of failures for the rest of his life.

What did he have to be thankful for?

"Well...I guess I'm glad to be alive and healthy."

Bill flashed a tight smile.

"That's all you need."

* * *

Julian returned to his mother's room about half an hour later, holding the Pepsi salad like an albatross around his neck. He shuffled past the bathroom until he could see the bed.

"Well?"

Sandra's special talent was imbuing a single word with a thousand expectations.

"I looked everywhere," Julian threw down the dessert. "That shoe is gone."

"Well, it must be somewhere. Surely you missed a spot."

"I checked laundry, I asked countless nurses and patients, I even went outside and dug around in the dumpster! And it was only when I was knee-deep in used diapers that I realized I'd gone too far."

"Well of course you had." Sandra's neck rippled as she shook her head. "The shoe only disappeared this morning, so if it wound up in the trash it would have landed right on top. You only had to glance inside."

Julian rubbed a hand through his ragged hair. "You know, the least you could do is thank me."

"I'll thank you when you find it," Sandra said. "So far, all you've done is run around and leave your mother alone in a room."

Julian felt something frightening rise in his chest. He had to get out. He spun on his heel.

"Now where are you going?"

"Listen, Mother," he said. "Someone stole that shoe. End of story.

And if they only did it to irritate you, then frankly, God bless them."

Julian closed the door, and walked down the hall, not totally aware of where he was going. He needed an empty room and eventually found one—a small lounge with an exit door. He beelined to the nearest trash can and kicked it, spilling the contents. There was no shoe.

Finally, his emotions died down. He looked at the mess and felt foolish. Once he'd cleaned it up, he pulled out his phone and video called his wife.

"Hello," Maria said. Her face filled the screen. "How is she?"

Julian's breathing slowed. Something about Maria's face, maybe the curve of her smile or her shimmery black hair, relaxed him. He collapsed in a nearby chair.

"The usual," he said. "I haven't even eaten. Someone stole her shoe, and she expects me to get it back. I don't understand. Why steal only one shoe?"

"That's weird," Maria frowned, moving to a quieter part of the house. The sounds of screaming children quieted. "Maybe someone desperately needed a new one? Like they got blood on one they were wearing, so they had to switch it out."

"Surely, they'd need both, or someone would spot them walking around with mismatched shoes. Besides, if someone was grievously injured around here, Mom would have heard somehow."

"Maybe they wanted to sneak something out in the shoe."

"They wouldn't need to bother," Julian sighed. "There's a door two feet from me, and no one's guarding it. I don't even have to sign out to leave."

"Then I don't know," Maria twirled a finger in her hair. "Could be you're thinking about this the wrong way. If no one had any reason to want the shoe, maybe they didn't want your mom to have it."

"That's all I can think of. She probably ticked someone off."

"No, I mean, maybe the thief gets some material benefit from her not having the shoe. Think about it…did anything happen because she lost it?"

"Of course, but that doesn't…"

It was like a trail of dominoes. When Julian thought about the result of her losing the shoe, he followed along to the result of that, then the result of that. He knew what he had to do.

"Babe, you're amazing."

"Am I? I'm not sure what I did."

Julian glanced at the time. "I have to go. There's only a couple minutes left. Next time I call, get Lily on the phone."

He hung up and launched down the hall.

* * *

Julian stood by Sandra's door, struggling to look natural while holding an uneaten plate of gelatin. He stared down the hall at the lines of closed doors. A few nurses fluttered around, focused on their tasks, and the hall was surprisingly quiet. Stale light shined from the windows of the empty physical training facility.

He glanced up as a door opened. Bill Dawes stepped out of his office and gently shut it behind him. He raised a skeptical eyebrow, nodded at Julian, then walked off. Julian smiled as everything fell together.

He slowly crossed the hall, touching Bill's doorknob. As he expected, it was unlocked. He stepped inside.

Bill had a fresh pot of tea boiling. His computer was shut, and his filing cabinets stood stalwart against the wall. Julian placed his dessert on Bill's desk and moved to the corner, just out of sight. He waited.

It didn't take long. The door opened again, and Monique entered, the light bouncing off her earrings. She started around the desk, then her eyes fell on the Pepsi salad. She stopped in her tracks.

"What are you doing here, nurse?"

She flinched and turned to Julian, her fists clenched.

"I could ask you the same thing."

"I'm here to get my mother's shoe back."

She turned to the window, a hand over her face. Her medical bag bounced on her hip.

"You've gotta be the most stubborn person I've ever met," she said.

"I think we both know where I got that from."

"How did you know I'd be here?"

"I didn't really," Julian stepped to the side, to keep himself between Monique and the door. "I didn't know you'd stolen the shoe or we'd end up in this room. All I knew was no one steals anything they won't get something out of. I realized that something didn't have to involve the shoe, it could be what my mother needed it for. Without the shoe, she couldn't do her physical training."

On a normal day, Sandra would be right across the hall, walking down that red line with the trainer. Though beyond the wide windows, the two would always be within sight of the door.

"I can't claim to know the details, but what I do know is you wanted to get in this office," Julian said. "I suppose Bill leaves the room unattended regularly around this time, probably for some kind of meeting, but usually there's someone outside doing training. With my mother out of commission and the trainer in her office, no one would witness you coming in and out of the room, except maybe one of the other nurses. I doubt they'd pay attention."

"You're really sharp," Monique turned to Julian. "But wouldn't it have been smarter to take both shoes?"

"You clearly know my mother as well as I do," Julian said. "She hates nothing more than throwing things away. If both shoes went missing, she would have declared it a lost cause and sent me to buy new ones. She might have been able to make her appointment. With one, she was stuck. She couldn't buy one shoe. Getting a brand-new pair and throwing out the leftover one would drive her nuts. She'd do whatever she could to find her missing shoe, but you knew she wouldn't find it in time."

"Maybe I should have busted the trainer's tires," Monique muttered. "Would have been easier."

"The only thing I don't get is why you needed to get in here."

Monique's gaze flashed to the teapot. Julian had a dark feeling in his gut.

"Why don't you show me what's in that bag?"

They locked eyes for a long moment, tension growing, but then Monique grinned. She held a hand to her mouth and laughed.

"Man, you're taking this way too seriously. Look, this is what I was gonna put in Bill's tea."

She pulled a cardboard package labeled with a brand name out of the bag.

"That's—"

"A laxative," she said. "I wasn't going to kill him. I just wanted to give him a bad day."

Julian laughed as well, partly from relief and partly from exhaustion.

"But why?" he asked.

"Bill turned me down for a promotion," Monique said. "I really could have used the money. My mom had the laxatives lying around. I wanted to feel some kind of power."

"I think I know what he told you," I said. "You should be thankful for what you have?"

"I've never been rich enough for that."

Julian watched the bubbling tea. He didn't think Bill deserved an evening on the toilet, but he supposed people looked different up close, especially when you couldn't look them straight in the eye.

"Look, I don't really care about all this," he said. "I'd say you're running a huge risk since you'd be much worse off getting fired, but maybe you don't want to listen to me. All I want is the shoe back."

"It's in my car." Monique grabbed her bag.

They left the building and walked along the parking lot, a concrete moat for the facility. With each step, Julian's thoughts drifted back to Thanksgivings with his mother when she was still a whirlwind in the kitchen, fixing so many dishes she must have had eight hands. As a child, he was baffled by the family members who flocked in and claimed to know him, people who had since disappeared when Sandra's health collapsed. For him, Thanksgiving was always their direct family around the table, light from the chandelier reflecting off brown gelatin.

He felt himself tremble under the weight of the memories when they reached a dusty two-seater car parked near the edge. Monique opened the trunk and pulled out the other shoe, its floral pattern a reflection of its partner. Julian remembered long ago when those shoes stood on the porch and watched him jump through a sprinkler in his swim trunks, as he flapped his arms to reach the sky.

It overwhelmed him.

He was grabbing at the edge of the trunk when he realized how fast he was breathing, felt Monique's gentle touch on his shoulder. His words came out as a current.

"I don't want to be here. I hate seeing her like this…She's the same, but she's so different, and it feels like a long, drawn-out, shitty goodbye."

"Hey, it's okay," Monique glanced behind her, looking for someone to take her place. "No one wants to be here. I'd be concerned if you were happy about this."

"What am I supposed to be thankful for today when everything I love has been taken from me or returned in pieces?"

"I get it. Some days suck," Monique bent forward to look him in the eyes. "You can't always be thankful. Sometimes what you lose makes you enraged, but that's only a reminder what you had was wonderful. I've met your mother. I doubt it was wonderful all the time. It's okay to be upset about the rain while also glad it's nourishing the flowers."

The Pepsi salad sat in the trunk. Its mottled exterior caught the sun in a way that enticed even Monique.

* * *

They dug a spoon through the gelatin, carving out chunks to drop on their plates. The remaining dessert looked desiccated and malnourished.

"Thank you, Julian," Sandra said. "I honestly didn't expect you to find it. When you came back from the dumpster empty-handed, I assumed it was gone."

"It would have been, if the thief had a simpler motive," Julian said.

"Maybe next time you should keep the shoes under your pillow."

"I can't even blame Monique," Sandra straightened her reading glasses. "I might have done the same thing while I was working, before I met your father. The girl's got real gumption."

Sandra ate a spoonful of Pepsi salad, letting it dissolve in her mouth. Julian took that as his cue to follow suit. The sweet taste of Pepsi was first to hit his tongue, accompanied by a high note of lemon. He chewed the pineapple and pecan and swallowed it all.

There are meals that drag you right back to your childhood, like the scene in *Ratatouille*, but others aren't so dramatic. You eat them and you're viewing a slideshow of every year in your life, the good and the bad, the love and the fear, the choices wise and foolish. You remember there's always something to be grateful for, even if only your memories. Sometimes it takes mixing gelatin and soda to get you there.

Julian stopped to watch his mother, wondered if she once shared a meal like this with her own mother. Though he hated to watch the world turn, he was grateful it brought him here.

Sandra swallowed. "After this, I really need someone to clip my toenails."

Julian shot her a warning glare. "I think you can survive another couple weeks."

Laissez les Bons Temps Rouler
donalee Moulton

This will do nicely. Chairs are spaced far enough apart to give people room but close enough so people can easily share a laugh with their neighbor. And there will be laughter. There always is when the vibrators make an appearance.

I've been a New Orleans Naughty and Nice home sales rep for two years, since I officially retired as Ruth Harper, attorney at law. Retirement is not all it's cracked up to be. I needed a little more structure to my week and a few more dollars and cents in my bank account. Naughty and Nice gives me both and lets me work when I want and not when an outraged client wants to rant about their soon-to-be ex.

Sandra Burton, the hostess, hovered. She wanted to see what I was pulling out of my bag of tricks. She'll be disappointed. The presentation starts with the "safe stuff:" candles, robes, diffusers. I suggested Sandra put out a few munchies. "It's almost time."

She grinned and headed for the kitchen. It'll be a feast of leftover New Orleans' Thanksgiving favorites: sweet potatoes with marshmallows, gumbo, dirty rice, and andouille. And there will be turkey salad sandwiches with the crusts cut off.

I reached into my bag for a bath crystals gift box and the box bit back. I pulled my hand away and looked into two brown eyes. I assumed the eyes are connected to the orange ball with ears that seems to have taken over my kit. Sharon is back, atwitter. "Oh, I see you've met Pumpkin." I have indeed.

Dogs are a pain. If they're cute and obedient, everybody wants to pet them when I want them (the people, not the dogs) focused on my merchandise and blissfully unaware of my 25 percent commission (plus bonuses). Dogs that like to bark or misbehave make customers nervous. Nervous customers spend less. I tried to think of a nice way to suggest Pumpkin be corralled to the main bedroom for the duration of the evening. Before I could utter a syllable, Sandra plunked four pounds of canine fur in my arms. The furball licked me.

So, Pumpkin will spend the evening with us in the living room.

* * *

Eleven women are scattered throughout the living room to look at merchandise that is lovely, but innocuous. They're here for ocuous. We munched on muffuletta pinwheels, fried okra, and warm cornbread as a precursor to the main fare. Pumpkin has been cuddled and cooed at. I've shown lingerie, pyjamas, bath bubbles, and massage oils. The aromas are heavenly, the quality is high, and the commission is great.

Sandra couldn't resist the urge to bring attention to herself. It was a classic hostess move, and fine with me. She went into her bedroom and came out, right hand extended. We couldn't miss the LaPearlite ring. It glowed in the candlelight. Sandra beamed. "Frank bought it for me. Don't you just love oysters?"

We oohed and aahed, but we all knew this was preamble. Now that everyone was relaxed, their curiosity stoked, and their thoughts on something special for themselves, I brought out the first of the erotic items: pink Ben Wa balls and lubricants in six fruit flavors. For the finale: the vibrators—bullet, wand, and rabbit. The women are beside themselves. Giggling and gaping. Pumpkin knew something was up. She ran from one end of the room to the other. Normally this would be a distraction, but somehow, she added to the carnival atmosphere.

It was time to spend money. When you sell sex toys, privacy is paramount. I don't take orders in the living room. I headed to the guest bedroom. Two chairs were already set up on either side of a small table. Order forms, pens, a credit/debit card reader, and business cards were in the middle of the table; product samples were on the bed within easy view and easy reach for customers who wanted an up-close-and-personal look.

My first customer came in, a nervous woman who quickly scanned the room. Maybe that's excitement. She reached across the table and handed me Sandra's expensive new ring. "It fell off her finger when she served the turkey sandwiches. She asked me to bring it in here for safekeeping." Pumpkin barked her approval and jumped up and up again. I realized she wanted to be on the bed. What the hell.

I put the ring in a small dish on an end table. I made sure my excited (I'm going with excited) customer saw what I did. That's the lawyer in me. Pumpkin barked her approval.

The night was off to a good start. Ms. Excitement made several expensive purchases. I do *not* want to know what this woman does in her spare time. Pumpkin bounced on the bed, and I began to share her enthusiasm. On closer inspection, however, my enthusiasm waned. Pumpkin discovered the wand vibrator makes an excellent chew toy. That will be Sandra's hostess gift.

Over the next two hours, Sandra's friends, family, neighbors, and other invitees purchased everything from kegel exercisers to lace collars and leashes to pheromone-infused body mists. We didn't do anything like this at Chastain, Boudreaux & Gaspard LLP.

It was finally time. There were no more orders to take, no more women with whom to discuss the intricacies of a nipple clamp. Sandra was starting to wilt. I suggested we do her hostess package later in the week after I tallied up all the orders. We could finalize her order over the phone.

She agreed. The dog! I realized I left Pumpkin on the bed. I apologized and ran in to collect the mound of orange fur. "She was a great help," I told Sandra, who was pleased.

"I have more friends. I'd like to do this again."

I gave Pumpkin a squeeze. As I was almost out the door, I remembered the ring. "It's in the small green fleur de lys bowl."

As it turned out, the ring was not there.

* * *

We were summoned. Oh, it was coached in pleasant-sounding tones and euphemistic language, but there is no doubt the women who were at the Naughty and Nice party last night are assembled for an inquiry. The missing ring has not been found.

Usually I'd shrug off such insinuations, but this is potentially significant for my business. I do *not* want to be the sales rep synonymous with missing jewellery. I arrived early, expressed my concern to Sandra, squeezed Pumpkin, and offered to help in the kitchen. I was told it wouldn't be necessary, Sandra's daughter-in-law, Ashley, was there to lend a hand. She's a lawyer. Sandra pronounced that with obvious pride and a hint of foreboding.

I've been here before. Hell, I've been her before. Ashley will ask us to sit in a circle, assure us all is well, and gently ask questions to determine who stole the ring. She will fail. Primarily because she doesn't have the experience to do this well, but also because her mother-in-law is watching, the ring may not have been stolen, and I am in the room. Ashley will have to be very careful about casting aspersions.

We were late getting started from the appointed hour. Not a problem, this was intended to reinforce the casual nature of the get-together. The china teapot and chocolate pecan pie, left over from Thanksgiving, reinforced this assumed nonchalance. Fifteen minutes later, we're ready. There are only five of the women from last night in the room.

"Should we wait for the others to arrive?" I asked. I knew the answer. Ashley called around. She thinks she identified the last person in the bedroom to see the ring. Anyone who was with me before was eliminated. They have an "alibi."

They really don't, Ashley.

The smaller number will be useful though. We'll be able to learn more and learn more quickly what happened. Ashley opened with a smile and a thank you. "As you all know, Sandra's ring has gone missing. We're hoping if we put our heads together, we can figure out what happened."

Etta reached over to give Sandra a sympathy pat. Rebecca tilted her head to send a look of commiseration. Pumpkin barked and bounced.

"Can you tell me the last time you remember seeing the ring?"

Each woman put on a look of consternation. They wore it well, and it may even be real. Except for me, the responses were unanimous. The last time anyone saw the LaPearlite ring was when Sandra flashed it around for everyone to admire. Ashley nodded as if we learned something. We have not.

Ashley turned to me, on thin ice now, but didn't know it. "Ruth, the ring was in the spare bedroom. Do you remember when you last saw it?"

I apologized for my poor observation skills but justified the oversight by pointing out I spoke with the guests, took orders, showed products, put the dog on the bed, took the dog off the bed, rang up orders, removed products from the dog. Ashley smiled. It was not as wide or as bright as her earlier smiles, but the corners of her lips upturned.

"Aah, we have a dilemma." Here's where we go downhill.

Paula wiped dog fur off her pants and suggested the ring fell out of the bowl. "Did you look on the floor of the bedroom? Under the bed?" she asked her sister.

Sandra huffed. "I looked everywhere. The ring is not in this house." In support of her owner, Pumpkin raced from one end of the living room to the other. She grabbed a chew toy and, well, chewed. The toy squeaked.

Regina picked up the chew toy. "Maybe the ring got put in a gift bag by mistake." She tried to be nice.

Ashely shook her head. Sadly. "I asked everyone to check. Unfortunately, no ring."

"Is it valuable?" Arlene asked. It's a smart question. Made her look innocent—she didn't know how much the ring is worth—and it raised the reason we're all cast in the role of possible thief.

Sandra looked affronted as if she would not be caught dead in anything that wasn't valuable. Before she could answer, Ashley leaned in. "More than $4,000."

I'm sure that's an exaggeration, but it's now the public discourse and will shape any insurance claim. This whole evening will demonstrate the value of the ring—financial and sentimental—to any adjuster unlucky enough to land with this case.

Etta, a large Black woman who has glanced at her watch three times since we convened, stopped mid-time check and looked up in surprise. "The ring was worth $4,000!"

There was a wide smile on Sandra's face. She nodded, delighted to be at the center of her friends' shock and awe. "You can see why we're so keen to get the ring back," Ashley said. She may think she was being delightfully Southern, charming, and coy. She was not.

Rebecca's the first to read between the drawl. She's not pleased. "You think one of us stole the ring."

Ashley tried to deny it but tripped over her tongue. To my surprise, I enjoyed the evening more than I thought I would. Still, I have a reputation to protect.

"We're all here to help Sandra," I said. Ashley looked both grateful and muffed at my interruption. Tough. I'm originally from New York. She can learn to live with it.

"Let's start with why the ring would go missing. Money is an obvious answer."

The women in the room are torn between outrage and elation. Nothing this exciting has happened to them in years. Still, what comes next will not be pleasant by any standard.

"You want to know who here needs money," Paula said. "Well, I don't."

"I appreciate the frankness," I replied. "It may not be necessary. I'm sure Ashley checked credit ratings."

Ashley did not. Her annoyance at my continued control of the conversation is obvious. "Of course, credit ratings don't tell the whole story."

Sandra's daughter-in-law is correct. I gave her a big smile. "That's why we're here." I looked at each of the women in turn. "We need you to be upfront with us."

"Arelene's husband lost his job." This is from Regina. The gasp is

Sandra.

"Regina had to get a reverse mortgage."

So, money is an issue. Ashley rapidly scribbled notes and looked jubilant. "Thank you," I said as I took Ashley's notepad and ripped out five pages. I gave each woman a piece of paper and a pen.

"It's a test. You have one minute." Every eye in the room was on me. "Write down the names of every pawn shop you know. Go!" No one goes. It took Ashley a few seconds, but she finally landed where I needed her to be.

"You're saying money wasn't a motive." Ashley gave up any pretext she was running this meeting.

"What else is there?" Sandra wanted to know.

"Who doesn't like you?" I asked and looked at Sandra.

It's Ashley who answered, aghast at my blasphemy. "Everyone likes Sandra."

"Then she is truly an exceptional woman."

"She's a pain in the ass." Etta turned to Sandra and shrugged. "Your heart is in the right place, but you like to lord it over the rest of us how much more you have, how much brighter your kids are, how much grander your life. It gets tiresome."

"Who else gets tired of Sandra?" I ask. Four hands reached for the ceiling.

Our hostess, the one who accused us of being thieves, wanted to wail in self-defence. There wasn't time. "So, Sandra can be a pain," I said. "Can't we all." It's the first laugh of the evening. Pumpkin joined in with a squeal. She found another toy.

"The question is really this: who really, really doesn't like Sandra?" I have no takers. I'm not surprised. People who truly dislike someone don't show up at their house for an erotic Tupperware party. With one exception: family.

Paula felt my gaze. "My sister can get on my nerves. I also happen to love my sister." Sandra is now in tears. Regina is patting her hand; Arelene is telling her everything will be all right. Etta makes more tea. I went to the fridge. Contention makes me hungry. Surely, there were turkey sandwiches left over from last night. There were.

If this were a Naughty and Nice party, I'd bring out the big boys right about now. Instead of laser-focused eyes and gales of laughter, however, people retreated into their chair cushions, eyes downcast. Two women talked quietly in the corner. Rebecca put her plate beside her chair and reached in her purse, I assume for a tissue. Pumpkin didn't care. Free food. In less than three seconds, Rebecca's turkey salad sandwich was gone. Pumpkin gave me a look. A swear she winked just before she licked her lips.

Ashley tried to bring us back together. We heard her but were unmoved. Literally. It's partly the weight of the conversation and the implications for future relationships. It was also most of us are usually in bed by ten and the clock was ticking.

I decided to throw a wrench in the works. Gently but firmly. "I wonder if we're looking at this wrong."

Now everyone in the room paid attention. "We've assumed the ring has been stolen. What if it's misplaced?" I looked at Sandra. She looked back. I won't be booking a follow-up party with her.

Ashley tried to play mediator. "We've been through this, Ruth. Sandra scoured the house. The ring is not here." Ashley says this like I'm four. Arlene and Regina nodded. Etta looked at me, tilted her head. "That's not what she means."

"What else can she possibly mean?" This is the astute litigator in the room.

"She means my sister likes drama." The women in the room smiled.

"She does like to be the center of attention," Etta said. The chuckles got a little louder.

Sandra was *not* amused. "Are you suggesting I'm making this up?"

She spoke to no one and everyone. She was hurt. I've done this, and I'm sorry, but it is a path we needed to go down.

Ashley bent over to squeeze her mother-in-law's shoulders. "No one is saying that."

"Ashley, read the room. Everyone is saying that." Paula wasn't holding back now, but there was fondness in her voice. She wasn't being mean for the sake of being mean. She looked at her sister. "Remember Dad's glasses."

No one knows what this means—except Sandra, and she knows exactly what it means. "That's not fair. I was eleven."

"San, we're all still eleven." Pumpkin agreed. She grabbed a chew toy and barreled across the living room floor.

Ashley is about to open her mouth. Regina stopped her. "Can we go home now?"

It was a good idea. We learned what we're going to learn. It was also a bad idea. Missing ring still equals Naughty and Nice rep taking a hit. I picked at my sandwich. Pumpkin bounced. I picked Pumpkin up. She ate my sandwich. I should have seen that coming.

Shit, it's so obvious. Regina's question remained unanswered. Ashley served up platitudes. I interrupted.

"Sandra, do you walk Pumpkin?'

"Of course, I walk Pumpkin. Do you think she never goes to the bathroom?" Sandra is angry. This has not been a good night for her.

It hasn't been for Ashley either. She echoes her mother-in-law in tone and content. "That really is a silly question, Ruth."

"Let me rephrase. How is Pumpkin walked and when?"

No one had any idea what's going on, but everyone knew something was going on. Turns out Pumpkin was walked first thing in the morning and after dinner. There may be a short walk during the day and a quick spurt of relief before bed.

"What do you do with the poop bags?"

Etta was there first. "Shit, the dog ate the ring."

"Don't be ridiculous." Sandra didn't sound convinced.

"Let's find out." Paula enjoyed this. Arlene grinned. "Do you bring the poop bags back here?"

They're in the garage. Two of them. One post-breakfast this morning. One post-dinner tonight.

There's some debate over who should examine the bags, but we all know it's Sandra's dog and it's Sandra's crap. The first bag is as advertised: one hundred percent poop.

Sandra gagged so Paula stepped up, snapped on blue nitrile gloves. She reached in the second bag and hauled out the first stool. She mushed it in her hands like cookie dough. Pumpkin thought this was great fun. It was not.

We're down to two stools. The ring was in the second.

Sandra was in tears. She couldn't believe her beloved dog ate her ring. She couldn't believe she accused her friends. Arlene said it was okay. Rebecca squeezed her shoulder. Etta gave her a kiss on the cheek.

It may be Ashley who saved the day. We made our way back to the living room. A pot of decaf coffee was brewing and a bottle of Herbsaint was on the coffee table (out of reach of Pumpkin). We sat, finished what remained of the sandwiches, and enjoyed our liqueur.

All was forgiven.

We packed up. Pumpkin got extra hugs. Someone made a joke about the shitty night we had, a good sign. When we can laugh about something, we've moved on.

Etta stopped me at the front door. "I'd love to host a party," she said. Rebecca nodded. "Me, too. I have friends these people don't know about." The laughter is back.

By the time my coat was on, and I said goodbye to Sandra and Ashley, four of the five women invited tonight booked parties. Sandra had her ring, and the love and support of her friends. And if Pumpkin was as good as I think, there's a turkey salad sandwich in the spare bedroom with her name on it.

Fruit Crumble

Combine the following in a large bowl:

¾ + 3/8 cup quick oats

¼ + 1/8 cup garbanzo (chickpea) flour or whatever flour is on hand

3 TBSP maple syrup or honey

2 TBSP + 1 tsp oil

*optional additions: 1 tsp spice + dashes of salt

Press the crust into the bottom of a 13x9 pan that has been prepared with oil.

Prepare another crust for the top.

In an 8 cup glass measuring cup or other large bowl, combine:

4 cups of cut up fresh, frozen or canned fruit

½ cup jarred fruit preserves

4 tsp arrowroot or cornstarch

*optional additions: 2 tsp spice + dashes of salt, lemon/orange peel

Spread fruit evenly over the bottom crust, then top with the second crust.

Bake at 350F until the fruit bubbles. Cool, then cut into 12 pieces.

Tip: Prepare the fruit ahead of time to allow it to set up. It can rest on the counter while the crusts are made, or be stored in the refrigerator until you are ready to make the crusts and assemble the crumble.

Great Aunt Martha's Pumpkin Pie
Sally Milliken

The squirrel kicked the soccer ball, her tail bobbing as she shot on net. The ball slipped under the fingers of the goalie, and the squirrel jumped up and down, sending her tail into a frenzy.

"Goal." I blew the whistle and raised my hands, or rather, wings, since I sported an inflatable roasted turkey costume: think human-sized golden brown cooked Thanksgiving turkey with a head.

At least I wasn't covered from head to toe in a squirrel or bald eagle costume for the annual Thanksgiving soccer game against our neighbors. After the exercise, each family returned to their respective houses feeling justified to stuff themselves silly. The winning family from the previous year chose the uniforms. We lost last year as shown by our squirrel outfits. As winners, the Fishers had chosen eagles to wear. I tried not to read too much into the options: a majestic bird of prey, our national bird, versus a rodent that runs around collecting nuts, forgetting where they bury most of them. No, no message in that. Whatever happened to team t-shirts?

The tradition of playing soccer had begun before I was born, the year after the Fishers moved next door. We shared a backyard—more of a hay field—which was the perfect size for soccer.

Even though I couldn't see her face, from the sound of the yelps, I guessed it was my brother Jack's new girlfriend, Jill, who'd scored. After the goal, our first, my family of squirrels high-fived and hugged, more of a bumping of bellies against each other, while the eagles flapped around in frustration, even though the eagles were up by three already.

One of the eagles did a flyby to circle my twin sister Julia. "Ref, she was offside."

She laughed at him. "Nice try, Trent." Trent was husband of one of the Fishers. He was charming and the only one bold enough to approach a pregnant former Division one soccer player.

It wasn't looking good for our family. I could already imagine the mortifying outfit next year.

On the other side of the field, Julia returned my wave. Under an identical turkey suit, no one could tell she was eight months pregnant. She'd wanted to play but couldn't fit into the squirrel. Just as well because it had looked like her wife, Sam, would self-combust when Julia started to pull on the squirrel suit.

I'd watched and bit my lip as Julia shoved her sneakered foot into a leg. She'd shimmied and pushed and sucked in, as she tried to zip the front over her large baby belly before she conceded defeat.

"Uh, Jules, hon, probably for the best. We're not ready for Baby to come, not yet anyway," Sam had said. She was too wise not to tell her wife, one of the most competitive people on the planet, that she shouldn't play.

I exhaled in relief, somehow agreed to be the second referee in solidarity, and then cursed under my breath when I realized someone thoughtfully picked up two roasted turkey costumes for the ref volunteers. Damn Fishers.

The goalie rolled the ball to Julia. I heard her grunt as she attempted to pick it up. I could only imagine how she felt. Even I couldn't see over the fabric of the large turkey breast and didn't have the large belly she did. She dropped the ball in the center of the field and whistled.

An eagle kicked the ball to a teammate, and the play began again.

We had the larger house, so we hosted Mom's younger sister, Lizzie, her husband Floyd, and their three children every year. Mom and Lizzie took turns checking the food. They made sure the house didn't burn down, or worse, the pies didn't overcook. In Massachusetts, home of the first Thanksgiving, we take our pies seriously. Especially pumpkin pie.

I doubt the Pilgrims made anything as remotely tasty as Great Aunt Martha's pumpkin pie: the luscious deliciousness of whipped pumpkin covered with a thick layer of fresh whipped cream inside a flaky crust. It melted on the tongue. The recipe is a family secret passed down from mother to daughter. Aunt Lizzie won't tell us the secret ingredient. Because one was not enough, she always made two. Others brought apple, pecan, and blueberry too. Did I mention we love pie?

Members of our parents' generation sat in fold-up chairs along the sidelines as they had once done every Saturday for years, to watch endless games of youth soccer, lacrosse, and baseball in rain and heat.

I lingered by the chairs to watch the game and listen to the conversation. Dad and Mr. Fisher had spent the first ten minutes of play guffawing over the players tripping over their own feet as they tried to kick the soccer ball wearing goofy costumes. Eventually, that wore off. When I tuned in, Dad was in the middle of telling a story for the second time. Mr. Fisher darted a glance at me, his brow furrowed.

I heard the swish sound of polyester rubbing against itself and turned as Julia stopped for a drink of water, her eyes on me. "Jen, remember the last time we dressed in identical outfits…"

"Sure, for a family portrait. You cut your hair because you didn't want to look like me. Mom freaked." I laughed. "You're in such trouble if you're having a girl."

She patted the material in the vicinity of her belly and smiled toward the field. "I'm looking forward to it. So is Sam,"

I scanned to where she was looking. Her wife was in one of the squirrel costumes. I couldn't tell which one, but likely she could. I could pick out the tall form of my husband, Amos.

She cleared her throat. "Have you spoken with Mom about Dad?"

I shook my head. "Not yet."

Mom's chair was empty, so I knew she was inside to check on the food. She and Lizzie were the queens of the kitchen. The rest of us were worker bees, told to chop, dice, peel, stir, and whatever else we were assigned. My hands were sore from peeling potatoes.

I sat in Mom's empty chair next to Lizzie with a huff, feeling ridiculous as the brown fabric ballooned around me. "How's the food prep going?"

"Oh, great. You know how your mother is. She has everything choreographed down to the last green bean."

"She's in her happy place. When do you leave on the cruise?"

"Next week. I cannot wait. Floyd and I have worked so hard." She closed her eyes as if imagining herself relaxing on the deck of a boat.

Julia blew her whistle, and the game ended. As the squirrels and eagles shook hands, er, paws and wings, I gave up my seat for Julia and sat on the grass.

"Watching you two run around the field makes me hungry," snickered Dad.

"Jen ran. I waddled," said Julia.

Amos unzipped his suit, pulled off the head, and kissed me on the cheek. "I'm hungry too." He pulled at the leg part of my costume.

I rolled my eyes and lifted my arms. "Help me with this thing, will you?"

He unzipped me.

Dad pointed to Julia. "Instead of a bun in the oven, you're having a baby in the turkey. A turbaby. Get it, instead of a turducken. A baby inside a turkey…"

"Ugh. Worst dad joke ever," she said.

* * *

Julia and I changed out of our exercise clothes in Dad's office. I noticed an envelope from a local bank in the recycling bin. Not the bank my parents use. Pulling it out of the bin, I opened it and saw the official-looking letterhead right away. I dropped into my dad's black mesh desk chair as I read the letter.

"Have you seen this? Do you know anything about Mom and Dad taking out a loan?"

"No. I'm sure it's nothing. Come on, hurry up. I'm starving. The smell of the turkey is making my mouth water. This baby wants to eat, and when baby is hungry, mommy is cranky."

"I noticed."

"What did you say?"

"Oops, did I say that out loud?" I straightened in the chair. "Listen to this: 'Dear Mr. Hanes, This letter is to inform you that, based on your lack of payment on your home equity loan, we will be repossessing your house on December one.'" I glanced at her and continued, "'Please remove all your positions and vacate the premises by then, or they will be sold and used to cover the remainder of your debts. Signed, Mr. Phineas Greed, Chief Loan Officer."

"I'm sure it's nothing," she said.

"I'd better ask, just in case." As the middle child—I was younger than Julia by eighteen minutes—I'd been nominated by my siblings to speak with our parents.

The TV in the den blared with a football game. I peered in. Our younger brother Jack was squinched between Jill and Uncle Floyd like a sardine in a can. Dad, Sam, and the cousins filled out the remaining chairs and floor space. Julia joined them. I hate football and chose to stay in the kitchen to help Mom. I knew I wouldn't be the only one. No one in our family could sit still for very long.

I filched a carrot stick from the appetizer plate. "What can I do?"

Mom shook a whisk at me. "Leave your phone in the basket with the others."

"I meant—"

She pointed toward the basket filled with cellphones and waited while I added mine. "Jack and Jill already set the table. You can stir the gravy."

I took the whisk from her. "Can't have lumpy gravy. That would ruin the entire meal. What do you think about Jack's new girlfriend?"

"She's a vegetarian."

"What's wrong with that?"

She sniffed. "Nothing. I just don't know what she's going to eat."

I surveyed the counter covered with dishes. Two different types of sweet potatoes, green bean casserole, mashed potatoes, homemade cranberry sauce, crispy roasted Brussels sprouts, and all the appetizers, cheese and crackers, and sliced raw vegetables. "I think she'll starve."

"She brought her own vegetarian stuffing and gravy."

"And you're complaining about that?"

"Her name is Jill. If they stay together, they will forever be Jack and Jill. Can you imagine their wedding… 'Jack and Jill went up the hill to fetch a pail of water…'"

"At least it's easy to remember." I added, "You don't think anyone is good enough for your children."

She shrugged. "Nothing wrong with that. You and Julia lucked out. Jack will, too."

I shifted my stance. "How's Dad doing? His health okay?"

"I've been a bit worried about him. He forgets things. He moves things around, then denies it."

Lizzie appeared and I couldn't ask for more details. Other members of the family rolled in and out of the kitchen to help, check on our progress, and steal samples. I stirred the brussels sprouts. Next to me, Amos mashed the potatoes.

"I'm ready for my turkey leg," Amos whispered into my ear and hugged me. "You are such a sexy turkey, I just wanted to eat you up."

I rapped his hand with a wooden spoon when I realized he'd used it as an excuse to reach around and pick at the turkey resting on the counter.

He pulled his hand back. "Ouch. Come on. The turkey smells so good it's criminal not to try it."

"Carving the turkey is Dad's job. He'll disown us if you start without him." I wagged my eyebrows. "Tell you what, I'll bring the suit home and you can unzip me in the bedroom."

He gave a low chuckle and rubbed his hand. "Kinda brings turkey basting to another level."

I barked a laugh and swatted his shoulder. "Don't let Julia or Sam hear you. And, that's not how it's done, you know."

"Who do you think told me the joke?"

I shook my head and gave him a hard kiss. I felt his lips curl into a grin under mine.

My grin lingered as he tasted the potatoes. He held out the spoon. "Do these need more salt?"

I tried a bite. "I don't think so. You're quite salty enough." I joked, but I knew what was on his mind. We'd been talking about having our own baby for months, as soon as we learned about Julia and Sam. As twins, it was expected we'd do everything at the same time. We'd been trying, and so far, no luck.

I noticed everyone else was distracted, so I pulled Amos into the office to show him the bank letter. "What do you think? Should we be worried?"

"It looks legit, but you know how many scams are out there." He used Dad's computer to search the bank website for the name Phineas Greed. "He really works for the bank. I think you should ask your father. And soon."

* * *

After the meal—vegetarian gravy and all—Aunt Lizzie and Uncle Floyd decided to go for a walk before dessert. I lay on the couch in a tryptophan coma and fell asleep. When I opened my eyes, Dad had disappeared.

I found him at his desk. No time like the present. How do I begin this conversation? "Uh. Dad, have you checked your credit report recently?"

"Not that I recall. Let's talk about it later. I came in here for a bit of quiet, to gather myself. We're having the best part of the meal next. I choked down your cousin's sweet potato with marshmallows so I could have the pie. At least the green bean casserole was edible this year…"

"Dad—" I restrained from stomping my foot.

"No shop talk today. Only family harmony and giving thanks. We have to make up for Floyd's complaining about his lot in life. Or discussing that damn cruise."

I sat on a wooden chair next to his desk. "You've already argued with Uncle Floyd about everything from whose hockey team was going to win the Stanley Cup to who had more knee pain in the morning."

"Well, of course, I tried every trick in the book not to discuss politics. You should be grateful. Took every ounce of control not to smack him on the back of the head. How your mother's sister could stay married to that jerk is beyond me." He sighed.

"That and Mom will kill you in your sleep if you ruin her holiday."

"That too. One year, Floyd and I argued over how to carve the turkey, and she had to hide the knives. Never approach an irate woman holding a potato masher." He touched his forearm with the memory.

"Seriously, though. I thought you froze your credit a few months ago after that last data breach with the credit card company."

He swiveled his chair toward me. "Jen, what is this about?"

I reached over him to where I'd left the letter on the desktop, tucked back inside the envelope. "I found this letter in the recycling. Is there something we should know?"

"You're going through our mail?"

"No, I went through your trash."

He scoffed and tossed the letter back into the recycling. "It's just one of those scams. Like the one where a family member is in prison and needs to be bailed out."

"Yeah, but Dad, you almost fell for that one."

* * *

After slicing up four pies and devouring most of them, we lounged with the wreckage of empty pie plates littering the center of the table.

Jack groaned, sat back in his chair, and patted his belly with both hands. "I'm stuffed. I must look like Julia."

Julia glared at him and scraped clean the empty pumpkin pie plate. "Aunt Lizzie, how much do you think we could sell this pie recipe for? It's even better than I remembered." She licked her lips.

Aunt Lizzie dropped her fork on her plate with a clatter. "For gosh sake, the recipe is from the *Betty Crocker Cookbook*. It's nothing special."

The room went silent.

Julia straightened. "It's not a family recipe, passed down from Great Aunt Martha?"

"No, it's not." Lizzie exhaled. "We don't even have a Great Aunt Martha. Ah, what a relief. I've been holding that in for too long."

"Mom, did you know about this?" I asked.

Mom shook her head. "As long as Lizzie kept bringing it, I didn't ask questions."

Hiding my phone under the table—I'd snuck it from the basket and had a healthy fear of Mom and her threats with utensils—I searched 'Pumpkin chiffon pie' and 'Betty Crocker recipe' and scanned the ingredients. Julia must have too, because her face paled, and she touched her belly. I guessed what she was thinking. The recipe contained raw eggs. What about the health of the baby? "Did you use pasteurized eggs, Aunt Lizzie?" I asked. Julia's eyes flew to mine.

"Of course, I did. Do you think I want to make everyone sick?"

Julia's shoulders dropped with relief.

I swallowed a gasp. Because one year we did get sick and everyone blamed it on the stuffing. We'd spent the night on the toilet, praying to the porcelain Gods. Those who weren't praying were sitting on the throne. My dad ended up with a fever and nearly had to go to the hospital with salmonella poisoning. Maybe it was the pie, I wondered. She'd never said a word.

Meanwhile, Uncle Floyd, who'd made the stuffing that year, had never lived it down. He'd been banned from stuffing for life. He hadn't seemed to mind, and at the time, I wondered if he'd done it on purpose. I'd heard of family members doing worse things to each other on holidays. Certainly would have been one way of getting out of baking and cooking.

I checked the list again. It also contained gelatin, as in, made from animal products. I couldn't remember which ones, but that was enough to know. We'd have to tell Jill.

A scream from upstairs interrupted the conversation. The only person missing was Mom.

Dad was first out of his chair. "Honey?"

"Mom? What is it?" I was one step behind my father. Julia struggled to stand.

Jack, Amos, and I tumbled upstairs and into their bedroom, the large king-size bed dominating the space. Mom stood in front of her tall antique dresser. Her jewelry box was open. She dumped the contents on the bed, the pile of necklaces a tangled mess. Julia and I knew it well, we'd played with the pieces as children, dressing up in her clothes, walking around the room wearing high-heeled shoes with our faces covered in lipstick and eye shadow, looking like clowns in drag.

Mom's eyes narrowed as she pinned each of us with her eyes. "My pearl necklace is missing. The one your father gave me on our twenty-fifth anniversary. It was here this morning."

Dad stepped closer. "Hon, perhaps you put it down somewhere."

She turned toward her jewelry box, lifted the top section, and held it out. "And my diamond earrings are gone too." She dropped the case and glared at Dad. "Where did you put them?"

"Me? I did not—" Dad shooed us out of the room. "It's alright. I'll talk to her," he mouthed, before he closed the door, leaving us on the other side. The door was solid but not enough. "Honey, I did not take your things," he growled.

Jack's eyes went wide. Amos, Jack and exchanged glances, and we tromped back to the kitchen.

"I'll make coffee," I said.

Julia appeared. "Is everything alright? What was the scream about?"

I told her about the jewelry. "What should we do? Do you think she lost it? Or Dad moved it and forgot?"

Julia's jaw dropped. "Oh, no. Do you think he's getting dementia?" She started to sob and leaned into me. "Maybe they both are…"

Jack muttered something about pregnant women being emotional. I punched him in the arm. He shrugged. "What? It's true, isn't it?"

I hugged Julia. "I don't know what is going on with Dad. Mom's healthy as a horse. Her mind is a steel trap. Just an hour ago, she called Jill, Josie. You know she does that to all Jack's girlfriends."

Jack shook his head and muttered. "I wish she'd find another way to test how they'd react. Large family gatherings are stressful enough."

I elbowed him. "You *have* brought a lot of girls over the years. I've got to hand it to Jill, though, she didn't bat an eyelash. Then *and* when we told her we were playing soccer in squirrel costumes."

Jack grinned. "She nearly won us the game."

"She may be a keeper," I said.

Julia nodded. "I agree. You're different with her than the others."

His grin widened.

"What about Dad?" Julia turned to me. "Did you have a chance to ask him about the letter from the bank?"

"What letter?" asked Jack.

"We found a letter in the recycling that said their house is being taken by the bank on December first due to a lack of payment." I exhaled. "He said it was a scam."

Sam and Jill appeared in the kitchen.

"Everything okay in here?" Sam asked. "Need help with the coffee? Your Uncle Floyd is getting antsy."

"We're discussing mom's jewelry. Whether she misplaced it. Or Dad moved it," Julia said.

Sam shook her head. "In all the years I've known her, your mother has never misplaced anything."

I began to put away the extra food. "The only other people who have been around are the Fisher family. We would have noticed if they'd gone inside."

Jill asked, "What about during the game? Does anyone have photos?"

Amos pulled his phone from the basket. "I do. There's one photo of us in our costumes, another with the heads unzipped so that we can see our faces. And some video. I texted you copies."

I zoomed in and counted the number of eagles. Nine. Seven on the field and two on the sidelines. "They're all here." I flipped through the others. "Odd, in one video, there are six players on the field, two on the sidelines. Someone is missing."

"You don't suppose one of them used the eagle costume to hide that he—or she—snuck inside?" Jack asked.

"It would have taken just minutes," said Julia.

Sam added, "Which also meant he knew where to look and what he wanted."

I shivered. "Mom accused Dad of moving her things, but he seems fine to me."

"Now what?" asked Amos.

"We can't confirm the loan with the bank until they open. In the meantime, we can look for proof," I said. "I wonder if the missing jewelry is related to the bank letter somehow."

Jack sighed. "We've known the Fishers our whole lives. How could they…*Why* would they…"

Julia clenched her hands into fists. "Which one of them do you think it was?"

I searched the photo. "From this distance, with the full costumes they look identical, you can't tell one person from the next. Check the photo with the heads uncovered, see if that helps."

"I still can't tell." Jack stared at his own phone.

Julia began to crack her knuckles. "Does it matter? It was one of them. It has to be. I say we go over there and confront them. Sam, get my shoes. Please."

Sam handed her the shoes.

Julia huffed and dropped back in her chair. "I can't reach my feet."

I coughed to hide my chuckle. My sister was going to be the best mom. She had the rest of us to guide her from becoming too much of a tiger. "We need to think this through. How did you hear Dad might be slipping mentally? From Mom?"

Jack shook his head. "No, Mr. Fisher asked if he was okay."

Julia's eyes widened. "I heard it from Mrs. Fisher."

"I overheard your Aunt Lizzie talking about it with Floyd," added Sam.

"Two of the eagles were discussing their money problems during the game," said Amos.

I sagged against the counter. "We've known them all for years, except one… Trent. It has to be him. What can we do to catch him?"

"If he did steal the jewelry, he couldn't have gotten rid of it yet," said Jack.

"I've got an idea," Jill said. She'd been sitting at one end of the kitchen island. We all turned to her, surprised. "Take the extra pie to their house. That'll give us an excuse. I heard one of them say they were eager to try it after hearing you all talk about it for so many years." Jill continued, "As a kindergarten teacher, I can tell when anyone is lying. Adults are no different than a classroom of five-year-olds. Instead of 'who dumped a bottle of glue on Maggie's seat', it's 'who's a thief?'"

"It's true," said Jack. "I call it her Spidey sense. I can't get away with anything."

He didn't seem to mind.

"We can say it's the prize for winning the game…," said Amos.

I leaned forward. "Or, a bribe not to repeat turkey and squirrel costumes next year. I like it."

Sam added, "Me too. We could spread falsehoods. Like, mention your mother's jewels are fake. Or they've sold the house and are moving. The papers are being signed on Monday. That would mean an irregularity would be discovered. Maybe Trent will panic and do something dumb."

"I looked forward to that pie for breakfast tomorrow," grumbled Julia. "Or dinner tonight. Or both."

"I was too," said Jack. "I guess we can sacrifice it for the greater good."

"I'll make you one. Now that we know the recipe." Jill snagged his hand and squeezed it. "A vegetarian version, that is."

"Don't screw this one up, Jack," I said.

* * *

We tried it as planned. Jack, Jill, Amos, and I would deliver the pie. We voted Sam and Julia should stay home. If necessary, they could distract our parents with plans about the baby.

We arrived at the Fishers, presented the pie, fanned out, and chatted with every member of the family. After half an hour, we reconvened outside.

As soon as the door clicked behind us, Jill crossed her arms. "Trent. Definitely. He's hiding something."

"Now what?" asked Amos.

We trudged back to the house. Julia and Sam waited outside.

I rubbed my arms to warm up. "It's getting cold, what are you doing out here?"

Julia looked at the front door and waved her hand and beckoned us over to a BMW sedan. "We're trying to break into Lizzie and Floyd's car."

"What? Why?" I asked.

Julia tried a rear door. "Because we can't find the keys."

"No." I scoffed. "Why do you need to get into their car?"

Sam explained. "They started to behave strangely after you left. Lizzie asked your Mom about the jewelry and blamed your Dad for its disappearance."

Julia added, "It was subtle, but she asked questions, seeded doubts about his mental capacity."

"She and mom get along great." Or I thought they did. "We think Trent is involved."

"What about a few years ago after Grandma died? Lizzie was furious when Mom got Grandma's silver set. She always makes digs about how little money they have. How can they afford a cruise?"

"I can't believe we're doing this." I went straight to the rear bumper and showed her the keys.

Julia smacked her forehead. "Of course, Mom and Dad's hiding place."

"Well, if we find nothing then they'll never know." Jack opened a door.

* * *

We returned inside to find Mom, Dad, Aunt Lizzie, and Uncle Floyd on cleanup duty in the kitchen. Amos, Sam, and Jill walked straight to the den.

"Cowards," Julia muttered.

A phone rang in the phone basket.

"It's yours," I said to Aunt Lizzie and pulled it out.

She waved me away. "I'll check later."

It rang again. "Lizzie, feel free to answer it," Julia encouraged her. "Mom won't mind." When she didn't move, I dropped the phone on the counter and pressed answer.

Trent's voice was breathless. "They're on to us. I must have missed a letter. Damn, I shouldn't have listened to you and taken the jewels. What're we going to do?"

"Hi, Trent," I said.

I couldn't help a snicker when we heard a low "yelp" and the line went dead.

Julia opened her palm to show the necklace and earrings. And two silver spoons. "Lizzie and Floyd, I wonder how these jumped into your car. Mom, I think you should check the silver."

"We found five bank letters from the past year." Jack waving the envelopes.

"Lizzie, what did you do?" Floyd stepped closer, his eyes wide.

"Nice try, Floyd," said Lizzie. "I'm not going down for this by myself."

Mom gasped and she turned on her sister. "You tried to gaslight me into thinking my own husband was mentally incapacitated. Why?"

"I think I know," I said, "When the bank repossesses the house, there would be no one to blame but him. I assume there are papers with his forged signatures."

Mom's eyes were wide as she examined the silver set. "Meanwhile, you stole the silver and replaced it with replicas."

"What did you do with the money?" Julia asked.

Lizzie flushed and shrugged. "I should have gotten the silver."

The cruise. Had to be. I shook my head. We should have guessed they didn't have the funds to pay for something so extravagant. "How did Trent get mixed up in your plan?"

"He caught me searching the mail. Said he would help if we gave him a cut. Idiot gave us away. In another year, I'd have had the entire set. You never would have noticed."

I watched Dad out of the corner of my eye. He made a call. Fully capable.

Three numbers.

911.

Then he ducked as Mom pressed the remaining pie, a blueberry, into Lizzie's face.

What the Dickens Is Going On?

Wendy Harrison

NYPD Officer Sumi Lin looked up at Santa in his sleigh, the last float in the Thanksgiving Day parade. The sun had broken through the gray, threatening clouds that hovered over the parade all morning.

It would be another half hour before the driver of Santa's float would get the signal to move. Once Santa got underway, Sumi was assigned to walk next to his sleigh, all the way to the end of the route. It meant she'd miss out on seeing most of the balloons make their way along Broadway, but she looked forward to the shouts and laughter of the children cheering for Santa. She was prepared to keep over-eager fans away from the float.

As she stood on the sidewalk, something brushed against her uniform pant leg. She looked down at a black cat whose green eyes flashed at her.

"Where did you come from?"

She bent to stroke the cat who had no collar or ID. Glancing around, she hoped to see the owner, frantically looking for the loose feline. Most of the people nearby were occupied with their noisy, restless children. No one showed any interest in the creature. Sumi picked up the animal who settled comfortably in her arms and purred loudly.

She examined her. "Girl, you need to find your way home. I'm on duty, and you don't fit the dress code." The cat licked her chin. "I'm really sorry, but I'm working here." She set the cat down in front of the bakery a few yards south of the float. With luck, someone would recognize her and take her home.

The aroma of pumpkin pie drifted through the bakery doors as people left with arms full of fresh-baked treats. It brought a flood of memories of family and laughter and tables that groaned under the weight of all the food. This would be the first ever family Thanksgiving dinner Sumi would miss.

"It's worth it," she told herself. "I'm finally police, what I've always wanted."

As Sumi made her way back to Santa's float, she smiled at the elves who circulated through the crowd of bystanders. All the promotions for the parade featured requests for people to bring canned food to donate for the Manhattan Food Bank. The elves carried sacks with donated cans that banged against each other. As one of the elves passed her, she saw him push something beneath the cans he collected. It seemed odd, almost as if he were hiding something.

She shrugged. Some imagination. She'd stood around doing nothing for too long. It was just like her to create a story to liven things up. In case her instincts were right, Sumi moved around the area, to pay close attention to the elves.

They all appeared to be males in their early teens. As she watched, she noticed how clumsy they were, as they bumped into the people who waited for the rear of the parade to begin to move.

"I'm not making this up." Sumi said it out loud. She talked to herself out of habit, one she hadn't been able to break, even after she became a cop. "If it looks like a duck, walks like a duck, and quacks like a duck, it really is a duck. These kids are up to something."

Although she could hardly believe it, a pattern emerged. Elf One bumped into a bystander and apologized profusely. She saw him slip something to Elf Two who then pushed his hand deep into his sack. Sumi stared as the hand came out empty. As she watched, Elf Two moved to Santa's sleigh and passed the sack up to Santa's helper who, in turn, gave it to Santa.

Sumi had no doubt she'd discovered a pickpocket scam run by, of all people, Santa Claus himself. "Ho, ho, ho," she mumbled. "You're busted."

She looked around for her sergeant. This would be her first arrest. She was excited, but not so excited she forgot the chain of command. Across the street, she spotted Sergeant Arlo Harris.

"Play it cool, girl." Sumi knew her eagerness as a new officer irritated him. She suspected it was worse because she was a woman. Swearing she would be calm. lay out the facts, and ask his permission to make an arrest, Sumi took a deep breath and walked toward the sergeant.

She ignored the hostile look he gave her and broke her vow to behave like a professional. The words tumbled out. Santa. Elves. Pickpockets. Under the cans of food.

"So, what do you think, Sarge? Do we cuff them now?"

He greeted her question with a frightening silence. His face glowed red with rage. She took a step backward and lost her balance. Her arms windmilled in a futile attempt to stop herself from falling off the curb. For a moment, she reached toward Sarge, assumed he would catch her. Instead, he took his own step back and watched as she landed on the concrete.

From across the street, an elf ran toward her, his hands extended to help. She debated whether to accept, since she was probably going to arrest him, but she was spared the moral dilemma. As Sarge shook his head at her wannabe savior, the elf did a rapid U-turn back toward Santa's float.

Sumi struggled to her feet and tried not to show how painful her back was from her fall.

"Listen, Honey," Sarge told her, "We're cops, not the Grinch who stole Christmas. You got no evidence for us to bust some kid elfs."

She stopped herself from correcting him. Elfs? It's elves. The least he could do was get that much right.

With statements from the victims who were bound to discover they had been robbed, as well as her own observations, even a newbie cop like her could make a case.

"Give me some time, Sarge. I'll find the evidence."

"You'll follow orders, Officer Lin. Or you'll find yourself looking for a new job. Now get back to Santa's sleigh before I substitute you for one of those reindeer."

Was he kidding? He didn't look like it, although his face was back to its usual pasty color. Only his nose stayed red. You didn't have to be a hotshot investigator to know why. The alcohol-filled veins were a dead giveaway. He would be a perfect replacement for Rudolph, not her.

Sumi crossed the street slowly, as to not trigger her back pain. Something wasn't right, but she didn't dare go over Sarge's head to the lieutenant. A rookie like her didn't ever cross the thin blue line that kept cops from ratting one another out.

Sumi found a stool near the sleigh where she could perch for a few minutes. No one paid any attention to her there, except the black cat who made her way from the bakery.

She reached down and with some effort, pulled the cat onto her lap.

"Still here? Don't you have a home?" She stroked the sleek fur as the cat purred.

When she looked back at the sleigh, Santa's helper caught her eye. Sumi couldn't help but notice the helper wasn't a kid like the other elves. The only part of the elf costume he wore was the green hat. The rest of him dressed in tight-fitting black jeans and a leather jacket. He was movie-star handsome.

She forced herself to look away. She might have to handcuff him before the day was over. Better to focus on that than to crush on one of the bad guys.

"Here you go, Fagin." The hot helper handed Santa one of the sacks from the elves.

"It's Mr. Kringle to you, Tangle."

"You can call me Oliver."

"Is Oliver Tangle really your name?"

"Is Fagin really yours?"

"Nah. One of them elves started calling me that. Don't mean nothin'."

Oliver laughed. "Never heard of Dickens? Fagin ran a gang of kid pickpockets."

"Like me, ya mean?"

"Yeah. Like you. So, what's your real name?"

"Pikes. Bill Pikes. Got anything to do with that Dickens guy?"

Sumi enjoyed the conversation. Santa just admitted he was running the thieving gang of elves. Good thing she had thought to press Record on her phone when she sat down.

Did she have enough to bring to Sarge now? Would she ever have enough? It didn't matter. She vowed to solve the case with enough evidence to force his hand. He'd be hard put to explain to the lieutenant why he'd ignored a crime that happened right in front of him.

Sumi slid off the stool and looked around to make sure Sarge wasn't watching. She spotted him in the alley next to the bakery. He raised a silver flask to his lips.

"Got ya," she whispered. Now she was sure she had smelled alcohol on his breath. She slipped away toward her car, which was parked three blocks north of the parade. The cat ambled along behind her.

When she arrived, Sumi opened the trunk and pulled out a red wool coat, her 'after the parade and I'm off duty holiday' way to be stylish and warm. Sumi put it on over her uniform and replaced her uniform cap with a warm red hat she'd knitted, with a scarf to partially cover her face. No one would take her for a cop. A rogue cop no less. She could get close to Bill Pikes and Oliver Tangle without suspicion.

"How do I look?" Sumi mumbled through the scarf.

The cat winked at her. Sumi sighed. Her small studio apartment could barely even hold her. She wasn't sure if she was allowed to have a pet. She started to explain to the cat she would have to bring her to a shelter, but she couldn't do it.

"Wait here." Sumi turned away from the cat and walked a block to the nearest bodega. She picked out a bag of cat food, two small bowls, and a bottle of water. When she returned, she filled one bowl with cat food and one with water. The cat stared at the dishes for a moment, looked up at her as if to thank her, and delicately ate the food and drank the water.

"What shall we call you?" The cat appeared to ponder the question but didn't offer an opinion. "I have it. Macy! We found each other at the Macy's Thanksgiving Day parade. Macy it is." Sumi put the empty bowls in the trunk.

She had an idea. She and Macy would find the proof she needed to arrest Bill Pikes and Oliver Tangle. She reached into the trunk and pulled out a bag of wrapped presents. For once, she had done her Christmas shopping early, knowing she would likely pull extra shifts over the holidays. She unwrapped a small box and held up the fake diamond bracelet she had for her mother.

"Sorry, Mom, I'll get it back in time for Christmas." It seemed like a tacky gift for someone she cared about, but her mother would understand. When she was a child, raised by a single mom working two jobs, she promised someday she would give mom the jewels she deserved. On her salary, this was the closest she could get. Mom would love it, even if it was made of paste.

Sumi slipped the bracelet around Macy's neck. The jewels sparkled against the black fur. No one would guess they wasn't real, and it fit perfectly.

"Now let's go catch ourselves some bad guys."

Santa's float still hadn't moved. Sumi cradled the cat in her arms and walked to senior elf Oliver Tangle, who was taking a break next to the sleigh. There were no teenaged elves around. She held Macy so the collar sparkled in the sunlight.

"Hi, Mr. Elf." She spoke loudly so he could hear her through the scarf wrapped around her neck and lower face.

He turned to look at her. "Hi to you, too. Are you playing Mrs. Santa?"

She started to object and then realized the red coat and hat might look like a costume. "Not this year. There wasn't enough stuffing to get the real costume to fit me."

Oliver reached out and stroked Macy. "Who's your well-dressed friend?"

"Sorry, ma'am." Sumi jumped as one of the young elves bumped into her. She turned toward him.

"Hey. Watch it. Be more careful." Oliver's tone was threatening.

When Sumi looked down, Macy's collar was gone, but she hadn't seen the elf's hand anywhere near the cat. She glared at Oliver whose right hand was now in his pocket. She was sure he'd taken the collar.

Before she could confront him and give away her hidden identity as a cop, Sarge pushed his way through the crowd toward her. Busted. He must've seen through her disguise. Being out of uniform was the least of the charges he'd throw at her. She'd sacrificed her career to show him she was smarter than he was. She deserved everything that was coming to her.

Sumi bit her lip to keep away tears. Women cops weren't allowed to cry, not if they expected to earn the respect of the men around them.

To her surprise, he elbowed her out of his way without looking at her. When he reached past her, she realized it was Oliver he was after. Could he have thought about what she said and decided to make an arrest without giving her any credit? She wouldn't put it past him.

"What the hell are you up to?" Sarge's face was even redder than when he had been angry at her. Sumi watched as Sarge spun Oliver to face him. "Ya think I'm an idiot?"

She stepped back to watch Oliver's face. He looked calm, but his voice was threatening.

"I don't need to answer that, seeing the scene you're making. Do you really want all these eyes on you?"

Sarge's head turned toward the crowd. Bored by the delay in the parade, all eyes turned to see if a fight was brewing. He dropped his grip on Oliver.

"Don't think you're fooling me and Bill too. You're skimming on us. I know for a fact you put your hand into those bags and make the good stuff disappear."

Sumi was having trouble understanding. Sarge was in on this?

"Sorry, Sarge. You got it all wrong. There's no need for any of us to get greedy. We're doing fine, just as it is."

Before Sumi could decide what to do, the bakery doors opened and the baker came toward them, holding four cardboard pie boxes against her flour-covered apron.

"You've all been so patient," she said. "I thought you might like some pumpkin pie. I sliced them up for you." She stepped toward Sarge.

"Officer, help yourself."

Macy took that moment to jump from Sumi's arms. She landed at the feet of the baker who stumbled over her. The boxes opened as they flew into the air. As the pies splattered on the heads below, Sarge glared at Oliver.

"Your cat?"

Oliver looked at Sumi and winked. She waited for him to point the finger at her. Instead, he scooped up the cat who licked his chin and purred.

"Traitor." Sumi hoped she hadn't said it out loud. She didn't want Sarge to recognize her.

Sarge wiped the pumpkin filling off his face. "This isn't over." His voice was low and nasty, aimed at Oliver and not her. He pushed through the crowd and crossed the street. Sumi wondered if all the cell phones raised during the pumpkin pie fiasco had posted videos online of the messy event. Sarge would be livid if he found out he was being mocked on the internet.

Oliver handed Macy to her. "I think this is yours."

"She thinks so too." Macy lifted a paw to pat her cheek. "I think you have something else of mine."

Sumi pointed at his pocket. Before he could respond, the motor on the Santa float began to hum.

"Let's go, boys and girls." The loudspeaker on the float vibrated. "Ho, ho, ho."

Oliver turned away from Sumi and jumped onto the float. He waved at her. "Until we meet again."

Sumi wasn't about to let him get away with the collar. She ran alongside the float with Macy bouncing in her arms, grateful the sleigh was moving slowly.

She shouted at Oliver as she tossed Macy to him. "Catch."

When the cat was safely in his arms, she jumped onto the stairs up to the sleigh. She paused to catch her breath. Oliver reached out his hand, and she grabbed it and let him pull her up next to him.

"What do you think you're doing?" He seemed amused, which infuriated her.

"Arresting you." She reached for her cuffs and realized they were under the red coat where she couldn't get to them. "Or trying to. Now give me back my cat."

"Only if you tell me what you're really up to."

He could at least have looked worried. Just because she wasn't dressed like a cop, he didn't have the right not to take her seriously. Maybe it was the pumpkin pie filling on her cheek, which he began to gently wipe off her face.

"Listen, you thief. I'm Officer Sumi Lin, NYPD, and you're busted."

He shook his head. "I don't think so." He turned his back to her and climbed higher in the float. "But he is."

She saw him pull cuffs out of his jacket and reach for Santa, whose hands were wrapped around the fake reins leading to the reindeer. The float continued down the parade route as bystanders fought for position to take pictures of Santa being pulled out of his seat and handcuffed.

Sumi realized the driver of the truck pulling the float had no idea of what was happening above him on Santa's sleigh as it continued to roll along the route.

"Who are you, Mr. Elf?"

"Detective Oliver Dickens, Officer Lin. Nice to meet you. But next time, please pick someone else's undercover operation to barge into."

FOUR WEEKS LATER

Sumi sat in her favorite bakery at a small table next to the window. She looked at her watch. He was late. He was always late, but she couldn't complain. Her hours were long but consistent. His were long and unpredictable. She wouldn't want to trade with him.

"Meow."

She stroked the back of the cat on her lap. "Don't worry, Macy. It'll be a long time before I can be a detective like Oliver. You'll still have me around when your bowl needs filling."

Sumi watched the steady stream of customers waiting their turn at the counter for breads and pies and cookies. It was the day before Christmas. She and Oliver were both scheduled to work on the holiday, so they agreed to celebrate on Christmas Eve.

She reached for her steaming mug of hot chocolate and felt an arm brush against her cheek as a small, gift-wrapped box was placed on the table. She turned to face Oliver.

"You could get shot, sneaking up behind me."

He moved to the other side of the table and sat. "But I didn't."

"Yet."

Oliver laughed. "Did you put in our order?"

"Of course. It should be coming soon. It's been a zoo here." She looked at the box in front of her. "I thought we agreed we'd skip the presents."

"It's not for you. It's for Macy. I'm sure she won't mind if you open it."

Sumi untied the ribbon and tore off the paper. She lifted the lid and pulled out a sparkling collar.

"Since you took back the other one to give to your mother, I figured Macy might like this one instead." Oliver took the collar from her. He stretched to reach Macy on Sumi's lap and slipped the collar over the cat's head. Macy licked his hand.

"I guess she likes it."

The two of them turned to the bakery owner who had come to their table with two over-filled plates. She put them down and added forks. "At least I didn't drop them this time. But what will you do when the season is over and we're not making pumpkin pies anymore?"

"I guess we'll have to arrest you for obstruction of justice." Oliver winked at her.

The baker laughed. "We can't have that, can we? I guess it will be pumpkin pie year-round for the team who handcuffed Santa."

The Bakers Roll Call

Shari Held is an award-winning fiction author, editor, and journalist who spins tales of mystery/crime, humor, romance, and fantasy. Her short stories have been published in more than four dozen magazines and anthologies, including *The Perp Wore Pumpkin* Volumes 1 & 2, *Sex & Violins*, *A Killing at the Copa*, the upcoming *The Great British Bump Off*, and *Gag Me with a Spoon*, all published by White City Press. She is a member of Sisters in Crime and the Short Mystery Fiction Society. When not writing, Shari cares for seven spoiled cats—three indoor cats, a neighbor's cat, and three ferals. She also feeds birds, possums, raccoons, the odd groundhog, deer, and anything else that shows up in her backyard—except the coyotes. She lives in the suburbs of Indianapolis, Indiana and attends movies, reads avidly, and enjoys watching tennis. For more information, visit her website, www.shariheld.com

Sandra Murphy has a head full of characters who put themselves into dangerous or ridiculous situations to make readers worry or laugh. They are dreadful nags who insist she write the stories as dictated, and worse, they all want to be in every story she writes. Those stories have appeared in *Ellery Queen*, *Alfred Hitchcock*, and *Black Cat*, all mystery magazines, *From Hay to Eternity* (a collection of stories), and in anthologies such as *Lunatic Fringe*, *Gag Me With a Spoon*, *Sex & Violins*, and more.

A known weirdo according to some, and far worse according to others, **Kevin R. Tipple** has had a lot of short stories published since the mid 1980s. That publication has often happened right before, to as much as two years before, a publisher ceased operations. So far, a few publishers such as Murderous Ink Press, Misti Media, as well as a couple of others have seemingly survived publishing him. He sincerely hopes that continues. His award-winning blog, now with more than 12 million page views and counting, features reviews, guest posts and more. https://kevintipplescorner.blogspot.com/

Vicki Erwin is a booklover. She worked in independent bookstores, for a publishing company, and owned an indie bookstore. She has also written thirty books in a variety of genres and age groups. Lately, she has been writing short stories like mad. Several have appeared online and in anthologies. Vicki's first published anthology story was also for White City Press, in *Yeet Me in St. Louis*. British mysteries are her guilty binge pleasure. Vicki lives in St. Louis, Missouri, with her husband (often her co-author) and her dog, Luna, who loves her taste in books—oops, loves to taste books.

Fedora Amis won the Mayhaven Fiction Prize for her Victorian whodunit, *Jack the Ripper in St. Louis*, followed by *See President McKinley or Die Trying*. Five-Star Cengage published her next two Jemmy McBustle mysteries: *Mayhem at Buffalo Bill's Wild West* and *Have Your Ticket Punched by Frank James*. Now out in paperback, ebook, and audiobook is *Vanderbilt in Peoria*.

Most recently, Fedora was a finalist in Missouri Writers' Guild's 2025 Short Story contest. The story appeared in *Yeet Me in St. Louis*, an anthology of humorous mysteries set in St. Louis.

Lisa Krystosek is a therapist, cheesemaker, and creator of everyday magic. She uses the power of story to highlight the ridiculous side of life. Perpetually hungry, Lisa often writes about her search for the perfect slice of pie. She lives with a rowdy pack of creatures in St. Louis, Missouri.

Mike Rusetsky is a Ukrainian-American author of horror, urban fantasy and speculative fiction. He started out as a playwright, with his original one-act productions *Angel of Death* and *The Plight of Smitty* earning critical praise. His recent publications include stories in anthologies by Outsider Publishing, Black Hare Press, Inkd Publishing,

Storm Dragon Publishing, Wicked Shadow Press and the periodicals *Sometimes Hilarious Horror, Tales from the Crosstimbers* and *Trollbreath Magazine*. Mike is an active member of the Horror Writers Association and the Science Fiction & Fantasy Writers Association. He lives in Columbus, Ohio with his beautiful wife and their spoiled Alaskan Malamute dog. www.mikerusetsky.com

Stephen M. Pierce, a marketing coordinator and Asheville native, reads so many mysteries he learned Japanese just to read more. Since writing this story, his partner finally tried his family's Coca-Cola salad recipe and miraculously survived. He holds the dubious distinction of breaking into *Ellery Queen's Mystery Magazine* before he landed his first full-time job which is more an indictment of the current U.S. job market than evidence of his skills.

donalee Moulton's first mystery *Hung Out to Die* was published in 2023. She's since published three more mystery books including *Bind* and *Melt*, the first two books in the Lotus Detective Agency series. Her short stories have appeared in Canada, the U.S. and Britain. In 2024, "Troubled Water" was shortlisted for a Derringer and an Award of Excellence. donalee lives in Nova Scotia, where they have grown pumpkins weighing almost 2,000 pounds. And no, the d is not capitalized. Don't ask.

Sally Milliken writes contemporary and historical mysteries and crime fiction. Her short stories may be found in a variety of anthologies. As well as bringing villains to justice, she enjoys bending clay to her will on the pottery wheel. She is working on her first novel, a historical mystery set in 1882 Massachusetts. Sally is a member of Sisters in Crime, SinC NE, SinC Guppies, MWA/NE, and the Short Mystery Fiction Society. (sallymillikenauthor.com)

Wendy Harrison is a retired prosecutor who turned to short mystery fiction during the pandemic. Her first story was published by Jay Hartman and edited by Sandy Murphy in the anthology *Peace, Love, and Crime.* Twenty-eight stories followed, most in various anthologies.

"What the Dickens is Going On?" is her 30th published story, again thanks to Jay and Sandy. When Hurricane Ian destroyed her home in Florida, she moved to the Pacific Northwest where she continues to write under the critical eye of Arlo, her rescued Shizoodle dog.

Lisa Lynn is the sister of J. Alan Hartman, Editor-in-Chief of Misti Media. The siblings grew up together with a love for the holidays, especially since those were the times when better food from the everyday fare was prepared. It has been Lisa's desire over the years to create healthy, tasty, and affordable versions of recipe favorites that also respect various food allergies and intolerances. Lisa is happy to collaborate with Jay whenever a publishing opportunity arises, especially since she shares his passion to give back to the community.

Lisa currently lives in the state of Georgia with her son Nathan and parakeet Cheerio. She is an after-school teacher and percussionist in a local orchestra.